THE
MOSTLY TRUE
ADVENTURES
OF HOMER
P. FIGG

RODMAN PHILBRICK

THE
MOSTLY TRUE
ADVENTURES
OF HOMER
P. FIGG

THE BLUE SKY PRESS
AN IMPRINT OF SCHOLASTIC INC. • NEW YORK

ACKNOWLEDGMENT:

With thanks to Richard Adams, veteran, scholar, and gentleman,

for gently pointing out the author's many errors and

persuading him to correct some (but not all!)

of the most egregious whoppers.

THE BLUE SKY PRESS

Library of Congress catalog card number 2008016925

ISBN-13: 978-0-439-66818-7 / ISBN-10: 0-439-66818-2

10 9 8 7 6   10 11 12 13

Printed in the United States of America   23

First printing, January 2009

Designed by Kathleen Westray

To everyone who ever lied and found

their way back to the truth,

KEEP READING.

1

THE MEANEST MAN
IN MAINE

MY NAME IS HOMER P. FIGG, and these are my true adventures. I mean to write them down, every one, including all the heroes and cowards, and the saints and the scalawags, and them stained with the blood of innocents, and them touched by glory, and them that was lifted into Heaven, and them that went to the Other Place.

I say my "true" adventures because I told a fib to a writer once, who went and put it in the newspapers about me and my big brother, Harold, winning the battle at Gettysburg, and how we shot each other dead but lived to tell the tale. That's partly true, about winning the battle, but most ways it's a lie.

Telling the truth don't come easy to me, but I will try, even if old Truth ain't nearly as useful as a fib sometimes.

The *P* stands for Pierce, which I got from our mother, Abigail Pierce Figg, that perished of fever and left me and

Harold under the care of her late sister's husband, Squinton Leach. Our father, Henry Figg, died of a felled tree before I came into this world, and when Mother passed away, our fortunes went from bad to worse, because Squinton Leach was the meanest man in the entire state of Maine. I tell a lie — there was a meaner man in Bangor once, that poisoned cats for fun, but old Squint was the hardest man in Somerset County. A man so mean he squeezed the good out of the Holy Bible and beat us with it, and swore that God Himself had inflicted me and Harold on him, like he was Job and we was Boils and Pestilence.

Squinton Leach. Just writing down his name gives me the shivers. Our mother was a kindly schoolmarm and taught us to speak proper, so I can't tell you exactly what I think of Squinton Leach, but it approximates what I think of a rabid skunk, or scabs on my backside, or a bad toothache.

Me and Harold tried not to take it personal because Squint hated everything. We just happened to be included, as he'd got stuck with us.

Once I made a list of the things Squint can't abide.

THINGS UNCLE HATES

1. HATES THE LAND HE WORKS, BECAUSE IT'S FULL OF FLINTY ROCKS THAT DULL HIS PLOW.

2. HATES BOB THE HORSE THAT PULLS THE PLOW, BECAUSE IT COSTS HIM HAY.

3. HATES HIS TWO COWS, BESS AND FLOSS,
BECAUSE THEY NEVER GIVE ENOUGH MILK.

4. HATES HIS HOUSE, BECAUSE
THE ROOF LEAKS.

5. HATES HIS BARN, BECAUSE
ME AND HAROLD LIVE THERE.

6. HATES WOMEN, BECAUSE
THEY DIED AND LEFT HIM TWO BOYS TO RAISE.

7. HATES SOUTHERNERS, BECAUSE
THEY OWN SLAVES.

8. HATES NEGROES, BECAUSE
THEY COMPLAIN OF BEING ENSLAVED.

9. HATES SENATOR DOUGLAS,
BECAUSE DOUGLAS IS SHORT.

10. HATES PRESIDENT LINCOLN,
BECAUSE LINCOLN IS TALL.

11. HATES THE SKY, BECAUSE
IT DIDN'T MATTER IF THE SKY IS SUNNY AND BLUE,
IT'S BOUND TO RAIN SOMEDAY.

Then I run out of paper. Parson Reed, of the Pine Swamp Congregational Church, he once said Squinton Leach was aggrieved of life, but I think he just flat out enjoyed being hateful. Enjoyed it the way some men take to whiskey or rum. Old Squint got so much pleasure from meanness that he kept on being mean, no matter what. And the worst of his cruelty got aimed at my brother, Harold, who was always sticking up for me and getting stuck himself.

That's how it all started, our true adventures, with Harold sticking up for me.

One day I'm feeding the hogs and Squint catches me chawing on a scrap of stale bread he throwed in with the slops.

"That's intended for the hogs," he says. "Not for the likes of you."

I keep on eating, wanting to get as much of it down as possible. Expecting to get pummeled and maybe kicked some, too, if he was in the mood. But when Squint raises his fist to strike me, Harold catches him by the wrist.

"The boy is hungry, Uncle. Truth is, we're both half starved. You feed them hogs better than you feed us."

Squint's face swells up red and bloated. He curses and makes to hit both of us, but he can't get free of Harold, who is scrawny but strong. Finally Squint trips over his own two feet and ends up facedown in the hog pen, covered with mud and worse.

That's when he really gets mad.

Me and Harold don't wait around to see what happens next. We hightail it into the barn and bolt the door from the inside. Through the cracks we watch as old Squint drags himself up from the mud and staggers into the house.

Inside the house is where he keeps his guns.

"He means to shoot us dead," I decide.

Harold shakes his head. "Uncle needs us to work the farm."

"Wound us, then."

"Whatever he aims to do, I'll stop him," Harold says, real firm and certain. Like he's discovered something about Squint and will use it to keep us safe. Like he's finally growed up enough to throw the old man down in the mud, if need be.

We wait inside the barn, studying the house until we spy Squint slinking out the side door.

Sure enough he's got his old flintlock squirrel rifle, but much to my surprise he don't come at us with it. Instead he marches over to the paddock. Next thing he's scrambled up on Bob the horse and off they go in a cloud of dust, or as much dust as that old horse can raise.

"Gone to fetch the sheriff," I say. "He means to hang us."

Harold gives me a look. "You know he hates the sheriff worse than he hates us."

"Where's he got to, then?"

It don't feel right, Squint leaving instead of kicking the door down and whomping on us like usual. Thing of it is, I'd rather take a beating than whatever he's got in mind, riding off like that.

Harold sees I'm worried sick. "Don't fret, little brother. I got a notion what we should do."

"Let's do it, then."

Anything is better than waiting for Squint.

Harold says he'll be eighteen his next birthday and the time has come for us to run away and make a life for ourselves. He says we can get hired in a logging camp and be logging men, with axes and saws and such. The way Harold tells it, I can see the campfires and smell the stew bubbling in the big iron pots and hear the rumble of green giants shaking the earth as they fall.

We'll ride great logs on big rivers, and get paid in gold dust and beef, and one day we'll own the forest itself and everything in it, that's how fine Harold makes it sound.

I'm chopping down trees in my head, happy as ever I've been, when Squinton Leach comes back with a crew of men to lynch us.

2

MUDDY
BLUES

It don't take 'em long to find us hiding in the loft. We're under that moldy old hay, holding still as rabbits when they bust down the barn door.

First thing we hear is Squint yelling and cussing and demanding they find us.

One of the men tells him to shut his trap.

"If he's only a boy, Leach, how'd he whip your fat carcass, eh?

Sure it wasn't a hog throwed you to the mud?"

Minute or so later the same man comes up into the loft, thumping the floorboards with the tines of a pitchfork. "Come on out and face the music, boys. It's that or get stabbed. On a count of one . . . two . . ."

At each count he thumps the pitchfork into the floorboards, making those sharp tines ring like a saber. *SWANG! SWANG!* Working closer to where we're hiding, as deliberate as an army advancing.

"Three!"

Harold gives me a nudge and we both stand up, clotted with straws of hay.

The man with the pitchfork is Cornelius Witham, that trades in jugs of whiskey and keeps a shack up in the hills. I recognized him from his voice, the way he said "throwed." Corny comes around on Saturday nights, leading an old packhorse strung with clay jugs. Squint won't take anything stronger than cider, but he and Corny share a fondness for plug tobacco. They'll sit on the porch of an evening, spitting and bragging on what they did when they were young. Corny is what they call a prodigious liar, meaning he's got talent in that direction, and me and Harold would hide under the porch just so we could hear him lay waste to the truth.

Only time I ever heard Squint laugh was when Corny told this long, complicated tale about a worm he swallowed by accident, and how it came out both ends at the same time.

"'lo, Mr. Witham," says Harold, picking the hay out of his hair.

"'lo, Harold. You boys sure stirred up old Squint this time."

"Yes, sir, we did," says Harold.

Unlike me, Harold never lied in his entire life. Which makes it all the more worse, what happened later, when they took us out to the yard. Squint's there, of course, looking madder than a bolt of lightning, and Corny that marched us to our doom, and Mr. J. T. Marston, the county magistrate, and a skinny, hollow-eyed stranger in a blue uniform so crusted with mud he could have been rolling with the pigs like Squint.

Man in the muddy blue uniform, he reeks of whiskey. His eyes are shifting everywhere but at me and Harold, like he's embarrassed for us, or maybe for himself. Mostly he studies the clay jug Corny must have given him, and seems disappointed to keep finding it empty.

"Harold Figg, you stand accused!" roars Squint, shaking his fists. "The boy tried to murder me! Put him in irons!"

"Oh, shut up, you old fool," says J. T. Marston, who has a way of speaking quiet but forceful.

We know Mr. Marston from town because he owns most everything in Pine Swamp, including Marston's Dry Goods Store, the Marston Boardinghouse, and Marston's Livery. Folks say he owns the law, too, and that's how he got himself named magistrate. Buy land or sell it, J. T. Marston takes his fee, or it won't be made legal and put down on the county maps. Anything you want done in the law, or outside it, old J. T. will see to it so long as he gets his share of the proceeds.

Marston has got a skinny white beard down to his waist and eyes as black as buttons. He grins at us with all of his yellow teeth, the way a dog will grin just before it bites you, and then he says, "Harold Joseph Figg, you must now present yourself to the conscription of able-bodied men, and take your oath, according to the Enrollment Act of March 3, 1863."

"Enrollment?" says Harold, straightening up. "But I'm not of age! I am but seventeen!"

"That's a lie!" roars Squint. "I'll swear on a Bible the boy is twenty!"

"So sworn," says Marston with a wave of his hand, as if shooing away a troublesome fly. "Sergeant, you will now administer the oath."

The stranger in the blue uniform isn't paying attention and Marston has to speak to him sharply before he staggers over to Harold.

"Are you ready, son?" the stranger asks.

"This isn't right," says Harold, looking from the stranger to the magistrate. "I'm not of legal age. How can you do this, Uncle? Who will take care of Homer?"

"I'm his guardian," snarls Squint. "I'll take care of the little devil, you can be sure of that."

"The oath, sergeant," Marston insists.

When Harold shakes his head, the stranger unholsters his pistol and holds it loosely at his side. "Private, you must take the oath or be shot as a deserter. What shall it be?"

"You'd shoot a boy?" Harold asks in disbelief. "I am not of age, and I think you know it."

For the first time the stranger looks my big brother right in the eye. "I have shot many boys," he says. "One more will not signify. Now raise your right hand and swear to uphold the Constitution of the United States of America, and the laws of the state of Maine, and to obey your lawful superiors."

Harold looks at me real sorrowful and shakes his head. "I'm sorry, Homer. Squint has got me this time. I must do as they say."

My brother is made to swear on Squint's Bible, and a moment later he's conscripted into the Union Army, to serve for three years or until he's dead, whichever comes first.

"Go with the sergeant," Marston tells Harold. "He'll sort you out."

"What about me?" I pipe up. "Can't I go, too? Swear me in, you villains!"

Corny laughs. "Villains, is it? Mighty big word for such a small boy. You get that out of one of your momma's books, did you?"

"Don't you dare speak of our mother!"

Corny shakes his head and grins. "Get back in the barn, son. Go hide under the hay until the war is over."

"I want to go with Harold!"

"Hush now, little brother," says Harold, giving me a quick embrace. "What's done is done. I am sworn and can't go back on my oath, no matter what."

But I kick up a fuss and fly at Squinton with my fists, and when that doesn't work I try to bite him like the rat he is.

"Cornelius! Put this brat in the root cellar!"

Corny takes hold and drags me squirming to the root cellar. The last I see of Harold, the stranger in the muddy blue uniform is marching him away barefoot, with a hickory stick on his shoulder. Apparently that's how they do it when you're sold to the army for a jug of whiskey and a lie.

I hope they give Harold a real rifle and a pair of boots. He'll need the boots to make it home.

3

THE WRETCHED LIE

MOST FOLKS KEEP FOOD in a root cellar. Not Squinton Leach. There's a stack of old beaver pelts that stinks to high Heaven, from when he failed to get his price and swore he'd let 'em rot, and did. Three wooden cases of empty Mason jars, now home to a world of bugs, and a five-gallon keg of cider that's gone to vinegar. There's some broken furniture that might have come from my mother's place, but I can't be sure because Squint never let us see it, and a pasteboard valise with a busted handle.

That's it, unless you count rocks and dirt, which he has in abundance, just in case he ever gets hungry and wants to chaw on a chunk of shale or granite.

Food preys upon my thoughts because the last thing I ate was that hunk of stale bread that was supposed to go to the hogs, and started off this whole mess.

It's all my fault. No question about it. If I hadn't stolen from the hog slops, Harold wouldn't have got took for the army, and it would still be the two of us against Squint, like always. I'd give anything to have him back, because the notion of being on my own scares me worse than spiders. All the bad things that have happened in this world, losing our parents and getting put up with Squint and such, Harold was always here, saying things would get right for us one day, and I always believed him.

He's not been gone an hour, but I miss him something awful. Plus I know what happens in the war. The newspaper prints a list each week of local men lost in battle, or from sickness. Never says how they passed, exactly, just a few words like "met his Maker at Malvern Hill" or "expired of his wounds," and mostly they don't come home, but are buried where they die.

Harold is so true and brave and fearless that he's bound to get himself killed.

Worried sick about what will happen to Harold, I lie in the corner feeling sorry for myself and for my big brother and for everything that's ever made me sad. Thinking on the dead and moaning ghosts and such, and wishing I had something to eat so I could forget about being hungry and concentrate on better reasons to be miserable.

Then it dawns on me the ghosts aren't ghosts at all, but voices coming from above. Squint and Cornelius Witham, bragging on what they've done.

I can hear them through the floorboards clear as day.

Corny's going on and on, about how clever Squint is, and the money they both made selling Harold to the army.

"Lovely piece of theater, Squint," says Corny. "How much did the judge take for his part in your little play? Thirty dollars? Maybe you mean thirty pieces of silver, eh?"

"Took his share like he always does," says Squint. "Can't be helped."

"Let's see, a two-dollar jug for Sergeant Harris, and twenty for me, for standing witness."

"That was the price agreed," says Squint, real stubborn.

"Which will leave you with a profit of two hundred dollars, near as I reckon. Once that wealthy pal of Marston's pays to keep his precious son out of the army."

"It'll take me months to collect," whines Squint. "Till then I'm out of pocket."

"But you will collect, eventual," Witham insists. "Not a bad turn of profit, for a fifty-dollar investment."

"He's my kin," says Squint. "So I get the lion's share. That's only fair."

Corny laughs and thumps his jug on the floor.

"Oh, Squint, you are a devil! Lucky for you the boy is so innocent. He'll be under fire before he realizes he wasn't sworn legal, and that the draft ain't even gone into legal effect yet. That was mighty smart, saying he was twenty."

"He could be twenty," Squint whines. "Look at the size of him. And besides that, boys younger than him have volunteered. Younger boys have lied about their true age and enlisted. Why shouldn't he?"

What they're saying makes me mad enough to spit, if my throat wasn't so dry. I heard the men at the dry-goods store talking about the new conscription law. According to the law, a rich man can hire a poor one to be his substitute, and die in his place if need be.

That's what Squint done with Harold, sold him like a slave for two hundred and fifty dollars, even though he's white and supposed to be free. Even though the draft ain't even happened yet, not legal according to Corny. So the oath Harold took don't count, because it came from a lie.

Soon as I hear that, I know what needs doing.

I have to run away from Pine Swamp, Maine, and Squinton Leach and his wretched farm, and find my brother and save him from the war, before it's too late.

4

THE DARK
OF THE WORLD

YOU WANT TO GET OUT OF a locked-up root cellar, think like a mole.

While Squint and Corny are busy jawing, I take a spindle from a busted-up chair and start digging around the stonework. Don't take long to loosen up a stone, and then use the spindle for a lever and pry it out of the foundation. The stone makes a pretty good thud when it hits the dirt floor, but Corny's telling his story about the worm and Squint is laughing like a dog that swallowed its bark and they don't hear nobody but themselves.

Then I'm digging with both hands, pulling away little rocks and clumps of earth. Clawing up through the dirt, quick as I can. Being mad at Squint and worried for Harold makes me dig faster.

The good thing about being small, I don't need much room to get through, and no more than an hour passes before I pop up beside the house with a nose full of dirt and my eyes gleaming in the moonlight.

That's exactly when Corny comes out the door, singing at the top of his lungs. I just have time to scoot behind a pile of stacked firewood and hunker down as he staggers into the yard.

"'No longer delay, love, I'm waiting for thee!'" he bellows, "'The moon in her beauty is beaming on me!'"

His voice is bad enough to crack the moon, but that doesn't stop him. Smells bad, too, stinking of whiskey and filth—he's that close. Drink has made him half blind, I guess, because he never sees me, but goes on his merry way, letting his boots find the ruts of the pathway home. Heading north, more or less, still singing about maidens and moonlight. Hard to know who's leading who, Corny or his packhorse that knows the way home.

Then Squint ambles out to the porch and my heart jumps into my throat. Figure he's going around to the bulkhead to check for me in the root cellar, but all he does is scratch his belly and yawn like he hasn't slept in a thousand years, and then he goes back inside.

Minute later the lantern dims and the house goes dark.

⌣

WHEN I WAS A LITTLE TYKE the dark scared me something awful, and Harold used to sit with me until I finally fell asleep. Might take ten minutes, might take an hour, but he never complained or made me feel stupid for being afraid.

Said it was what our Dear Mother would have wanted, and he was glad of the chance to oblige.

Dark doesn't bother me as much as it used to, but I can't say it pleases me, neither. In the dark I feel the eyes of the forest upon me, and it keeps my heart thumping so hard and fast my ears are hot. Part of me wants to crawl back into the cellar and hide, but I know there's no turning back.

After a while old Squint commences to snore, which he does so loud and fruitful you could hear it in the next county, never mind from behind the woodpile.

It's now or never, so I get up from behind the woodpile and head for the paddock where Squint left the horse.

The way I figure, our Dear Mother would want me to save Harold from getting killed in the war, just like she wanted him to keep me from being scared of the dark. Can't catch up to him on foot, so it stands to reason she'd want me to take Bob the horse even if some folks might consider it stealing. Fact is, old Bob came to Squint as part of my mother's estate, so I have a prior attachment, even if it's not exactly legal.

Bob doesn't mind. He comes over and nuzzles at my hand, soon as I duck into the paddock. Always does that, even though I never once had an apple or a lump of sugar to give him. Could be he recognizes my smell, or maybe he just likes the company.

"Hey, Bob," I whisper. "Want to go for a walk tonight? Good horse. Shush. Easy now."

Squint left the bridle on him and the only saddle the horse has ever known is an old blanket, so it doesn't take but a moment to lead him out of the paddock and away from the house. Seems like we're making a dreadful racket, with clattering hooves and me tripping over rocks and such, and that we'll wake the dead and Squint, too.

He never does awaken, and by the time me and Bob get over the first hill the moon is down and the dark of the world is all around us. A few stars show through the racing clouds, and that's enough to point me south, and follow in my brother's footsteps, even if I can't exactly see 'em.

Figure to get as many miles away as possible before the sun rises. Squint is sure to follow, if only to get back his horse, and this time he really will have murder in mind.

5

BEARS AS BIG
AS BOULDERS

YOU PROBABLY ALREADY know this, but horses don't like to go places at night, any more than sensible folks do. A horse has his patterns and his habits, and night is for standing around and sleeping. For a while Bob keeps trying to turn back, his eyes rolling white and fearful, but he doesn't fight me too much, all things considered.

"Good horse," I keep telling him. Mostly so I can hear the sound of my own voice, because the forest has a way of creaking and groaning that puts a lump of nothing in my stomach.

It's only the tall trees, I keep telling myself. The pine and spruce and hackmatack moving in the wind. The way their long boughs brush like fingers, and make a sighing you can feel deep in your bones.

"Good horse," I say. "Good horse."

It's not like we're moving fast. Bob's old and slow, and

besides, even a young horse can't run in the dark or he'll break a leg for sure. Has to see the ground or he doesn't feel connected.

I walk Bob for miles, and then skinny up onto his back and let him walk me for a while. Under the night shadows of the mighty trees, finding our path through the blind darkness, me and that good old horse.

All the time Harold is in my mind, how he must have marched and marched with the stick on his shoulder and the whiskey sergeant shouting orders. Does it scare him to be that far from home? Does he know I might follow? Do his feet hurt? Then I get to fussing that bears might get him, black bears as big as boulders, and it makes me so fearful that the shadows start to look like hungry bears, and the spruce branches are the bears' long teeth, snapping at us from behind.

Bob the horse, he knows I'm afraid and that makes him afraid, too, and he starts to pick up the pace.

"Whoa, now, hold!"

I pull back on the reins but the horse won't stop. He's got an idea in his head and the idea is to run away from the darkness and the shadows. Run until he gets to daylight and can see the world again.

All I can do is hang on, clinging to his thick neck. Branches whipping all around us, so close I can smell the pine needles. The horse snorting with fear and shaking his head to keep clear of the reins. Running blind at a full gallop, trusting his hooves to find the way. Not caring what the next step brings.

Figure any second he'll trip and break a leg and I'll go flying and crack my skull on the trees or the rocks, and that will be the end of my adventure. But just as fast as he bolted, Bob starts to slow down. He's run out of oats and remembered how old he is, and that he can't run that fast no more, and he's heaving and gasping and snorting up a lather.

Got to rest the horse or he'll die on me, for certain. Poor old thing is shaking, he's so wrung out, and making funny little noises deep in his throat that mean he's still plenty scared.

Me, too. Because I can hear something in the dark that shouldn't be there. Voices. Folks talking. Two men, sounds like. One of 'em low and rumbly so the words are muffled, but the other voice, the one that's doing all the telling, that voice is clear as a bell.

"Kill that son of a bee," it says. "Kill him while we got the chance."

6

THE WORST SMELL EVER

"IF WE KILL HIM NOW, we never get our money."

"Come on, Stink. Why'd you want to spoil all my fun? You know we got to dispatch him eventual."

"Back away afore I lose my temper, Smelt. Ain't you got no sense?"

Stink and Smelt. Pair of cold-blooded killers arguing in the woods, close enough to hear my heart beating. To make matters worse, the night is fading fast. Never thought I'd want the dark to last longer, but times like this, the light of day will catch me sure as Christmas.

What gives me away isn't daylight, though. It's Bob the horse, deciding to whinny.

"Hold on! You hear that?"

A moment later a big man comes crashing out of the spruce trees and catches me trying to hide behind the horse. The big man is missing an eyeball that's got an empty socket, but apparently he can see me fine with his one good eye.

"Step away from that nag, boy!"

Before I can move an inch the big man picks me off the ground and holds me up like a sack of beans. Gives me a shake and bellows, "You spyin' for the judge, boy? He send you out here?"

Once in the heat of summer an old rooster got up in the hay and died, and Harold and me thought it was the worst smell ever, but that's before I made the acquaintance of Stink Mullins. Every part of him smells of rot. His black teeth, his scabby eye socket, his crusty beard, all of it makes a sick hog's fart smell sweet by comparison.

Odor so overpowering I can't hardly breathe, let alone defend myself against the charge of being a spy for the judge. What judge? What spy? Have I got to the war already?

"Huh? What do you say, boy?"

Before I can answer he drops me to the ground and all the air woofs out of me.

"What's this?"

The other man, the one called Smelt, is a whole lot smaller and skinnier and less fragrant, but he's got all the charm of an energetic weasel. There he is, circling around as if he's looking for a place to bite. When he prods me with a boot I grab hold of his foot, to stop him from kicking.

He snarls and shakes me off.

"Where'd he come from?" he wants to know.

"Where you from, boy?" Stink demands.

When I get my breath back I tell him the general area,

without mentioning Squint or his farm, in case he's already raised an alarm.

"In the area of Pine Swamp, is that right?" Stink says.

"Near abouts," I admit. "That's the closest town."

"Then the judge sent you, like I figured."

"Nobody sent me," I tell him. "I'm just lost in the woods, is all."

"He's lyin'," says Smelt, crouching down to look me in the eye. "You the judge's boy, that's who you are."

"I'm Homer Figg. Let go my ear. It hurts."

Both men laugh.

"Ear won't hurt none when we cut it off," says Smelt, reaching for his knife.

"Hold now," Stink says. "The boy can't hear us with an ear off."

"Let me take his tongue," Smelt insists. "Can't lie if he ain't got no tongue."

"Homer Figg," Stinks says, rubbing at his beard. "Figg, Figg, Figg. Wait now. I knew a Henry Figg once. He kin of yours?"

"My father," I tell him.

Stink sneers at me. His smelly breath makes my eyes water worse than a moldy onion. "Is that right?" he says. "If he really was your kin then I expect you'll know how he died."

"Died of a felled tree," I say.

"Never liked the man," Stink says, satisfied. "Thought he knew everything, but he didn't know that tree, did he?"

Stink carries me through the woods to where they've built a lean-to shelter out of spruce boughs. There's a man inside, trussed up like a hog, his head covered with a burlap flour sack.

"Best tie him up, too."

Smelt lashes my wrists and ankles with a rawhide strip while Stink collects Bob the horse.

The man with the sack on his head moans and tries to work himself free. Smelt kicks him, and the man goes silent, as if holding himself still inside.

"That's better," Smelt says to the man with the sack on his head. "You stay quiet as a mouse, maybe you'll live to see the sun come up. Which is any minute now."

Smelt turns his attention to me. Crouches down, grinning. He's only got one tooth and he keeps touching it with his tongue while he studies me, like a toad studies a fly. "If you're really from Pine Swamp, I expect you know the local judge, Mr. J. T. Marston."

"Course I know him. He sold my brother into the army."

Smelt's hard little eyes brighten like bits of black glass. "Hmm. Sounds like somethin' J. T. would do," he says, rubbing at his jaw. "The judge'd sell his own mother for a barrel of sour pickles."

"Please let me go," I beg, trying to sound pitiful, which isn't too hard under the circumstances.

"Why'd I do that?" Smelt wants to know.

"Let me go and I'll see that you are amply rewarded. My rich uncle will pay you a hundred in gold."

Smelt likes the idea. "You got a rich uncle, do you? How rich?"

"Richest man in Maine. Owns all the trees in three counties, and most of the grass. Owns his own railroad, and all the cars and engines. A hundred in gold is nothing to him."

"Uh-huh. And what exactly are you doing out here in these woods your rich uncle owns?"

"I've got to find my brother afore he gets killed in the war."

Smelt finds that amusing. "You and your rich uncle gonna buy him out of the Union Army, are you? I checked your pockets, boy. You ain't got no money. Not one red cent. You don't have a saddle and you don't have shoes. All you had was an old nag ain't hardly good enough for glue. And we aim to keep that horse, for the trouble you caused us."

"That makes you a horse thief," I tell him.

Smelt slaps my face. Not too hard, just enough to make me cringe. "Watch what you call a man! Horse thieves are for hanging. Call me a thief, but have you got any papers to prove you own that bag of bones?"

"Yes, sir. Piles of papers. Deeds and bills of sale and proof of ownership."

"Hid them in the woods, I suppose, all those papers?"

"No, sir. Left 'em in the safe in my uncle's bank."

"Uh-huh. You're a pretty fair liar, ain't you, boy? Look me in the eye and tell me you really got papers."

I look him in the eye and say, "I've got papers. It's my horse, fair and legal."

"Hmm. That's good. Average man might believe you, but I expect you stole that nag from some poor farmer."

"No, sir! It was my father's horse, and left to my Dear Mother until she died. It should belong to me and my brother."

Smelt nods to himself, like he knew I was fibbing all along. "'Should be' is a different thing than 'is.' Forget the horse, boy. Figure how you can be useful. That's what'll keep you alive." Stink comes into the lean-to holding his hand that's bleeding.

"Horse took a bite out of me," he announces, sounding surprised.

"What'd you do?" Smelt wants to know.

"I bit him back."

"You want to be careful, Stink, biting on a horse. It's bad for your teeth."

"That how you lost yours?" Stink asks, sneering.

But Smelt ignores him and licks his one remaining tooth, as if deep in thought. "Whilst you was biting horses, I come upon an idea," he says. "I think there's a way we can use this boy."

"Use him? He ain't hardly big enough to dig his own grave."

"No," says Smelt, "but he's a prodigious good liar. Ain't you, Homer Figg?"

Comes to me that I better tell the truth, or they'll find a way to make me dig my own grave.

"Yes, sir," I admit. "I'm a real good liar."

7

THE MAN
IN THE SACK

I ONCE TOLD PARSON REED of the Pine Swamp Congregational Church that my mother and father were not
dead, but away visiting Queen Victoria, and that they
would soon be sending for me and Harold. The parson was
powerfully impressed that a boy of five knew the queen by
name, and even more impressed when I explained that my
father had been hired to fell all the trees in England, and
that the task would take no more than a week. The parson
said he'd not been aware that so few trees remained in the
British Empire, and I explained that my father could fell a
tree with one swing of his ax, and could therefore lay an
entire forest down in an hour or so, depending on his mood.
And while my father was laying waste to the forests my
mother was busy in the royal palace, teaching the queen
how to spell.

When Parson Reed said it was a great surprise to learn

the queen could not spell, I explained that until recently kings and queens had no need of spelling or reading, because servants did it for them, and the parson remarked that I had a surprising knowledge of the world for a child of my age, or any age for that matter.

The kindly parson may have been amused by my inventions, but my brother was not. He told me our Dear Mother had made him swear he would always be truthful, and that his oath extended to me, even if I'd been too young to swear it myself, and that every time I told a lie an angel fell from Heaven.

For days after that I went around looking for fallen angels, but never encountered one, so I come to believe my big brother must have been mistaken, even if he did believe such a thing. But as strict as he can be about never lying, I'm pretty sure Harold won't mind if I bend the truth to stay alive.

Of course, that's before I find out what they want me to lie about.

First thing Smelt does is force the prisoner to sit up. There's something pitiful about a man with a sack on his head. Knowing he can't see what's going to happen next, and how every little noise makes him flinch. The light of dawn has come into the lean-to shelter and I can see the man's hands are all swollen black from where he's been tied up.

"You hear me in there, Festus?" Smelt demands. "Count

of three I'm cutting off this sack, and if you don't want your head cut off, too, you better tell us what we want to know."

Out of Smelt's wide leather belt comes a thick-bladed knife with a wicked curve, just right for slicing a hog's throat, or a man's. He slips the shining blade up under the flour sack and slices it open with one flick of his wrist. The sack falls away and I'm looking at two white eyes as big as saucers. Two white eyes in a face the color of creamed coffee.

"Festus is our darky friend, ain't you, Festus?"

The white eyes squint up at Smelt and I can tell the darky man is fearful but he's angry, too. "I ain't Festus," he says. "Never was."

"You're Festus if we say so," Stink insists, waving his fist in the man's face.

The man gives his head a stubborn shake and glares up at Stink. "My name is Samuel Reed and I am a free man, born to a free woman in the state of Rhode Island!"

Smelt slowly crouches down, holding the big knife. He smiles in a way that makes me feel sick to my stomach. If a snake could smile it would look just like him. "This ain't Rhode Island," he says, "and we don't care who you was born to, or where you got the crazy notion that a darky can talk the same as a white man. All we care about is this. Tell us where you hid them runaway slaves."

"They are not slaves!" the man insists. "They have been set free by President Lincoln."

"Yeah? If they ain't slaves no more, why they running away?"

The man refuses to answer. The way he's keeping still and quiet, it's as if he expects to die before the sun gets much higher. Might be he's praying, too, without saying the words aloud.

"Best get it over with," Stink suggests.

"Last chance," Smelt says, pointing with his knife. "Speak or meet your Maker."

The darky man gives his head a little shake. You can tell he's scared of the knife, and doesn't want to die, but he won't say where the runaway slaves are hid, even if it kills him.

I'm scared of that knife, too, but something in me needs to pipe up, and I can't stop my mouth from saying, "You might just as well throw your money in a hole in the ground!"

"What?"

Smelt and Stink turn their attention to me.

"You can't sell this man if he's dead," I point out.

Stink looks as if he's fixing to punch me, but Smelt stops him. "Hold on," he says. "The boy may have a point. We could forge owner papers easy enough, and collect the bounty."

"Bounty?" I ask, figuring the more talk, the less call for a knife.

"Ten dollar bounty for every slave returned to Maryland," Smelt tells me. "Emancipation don't cover the border states. That's a legal fact."

They're talking about the Emancipation Proclamation. I heard men arguing about it down at the general store, where they smoke and chaw of a Saturday afternoon.

Seems like when President Lincoln declared that slaves in the Confederacy were free, he didn't dare free the slaves in Union states like Maryland, Delaware, or Kentucky, in fear the border states might join the rebels. The proclamation is more like what they call a promise to the future, when the war has been won. Don't count for much now, not if you're a slave.

Smelt and Stink get to talking and decide they'll leave the darky man alive for now, at least until the boy helps them locate where the runaway slaves are hid. The boy who's going to lie his way onto the Underground Railroad. The boy who's going to make them rich.

Must be that being scared makes you stupid, because it takes a while for me to realize the boy is me.

———

STINK MULLINS TAKES CHARGE of Samuel Reed, the darky man, while me and Smelt head off into the pine forest, looking for a trail.

He's tied a rope around my neck, like you would with a mule or a dog, and if I pull too hard the rope tightens.

"You're a quick little fella," he says. "Best keep in mind you can't outrun my knife."

To demonstrate, he flicks his knife at a tree trunk and hits it square in the middle, with the blade buried deep.

There may come a time when I can get loose and run for it, but for now I'm going along, doing what he says. Walking through the soft leaves, smelling the spruce and pine all around us, and the ferns that tickle my knees.

About a mile from the lean-to camp we finally come upon the trail. By the look of it, wagons and horses have passed by recently. Smelt rubs his scraggly beard and nods to himself and says, "We ain't got that far to go, so we best get your story straight."

"My story?"

"Who you're pretending to be. Family hiding the fugitives is Brewster," he says, as if expecting me to be impressed. "You heard of the Brewster Mines?"

I shake my head.

"Ain't heard of much, have you? Jebediah Brewster come here from Pennsylvania and made a fortune in gemstones. Now he's selling lead and copper to the army and using the money to send slaves to Canada, where they can't be touched. I know for a fact the old man has got thirty fugitives hid somewhere on his property but I don't know where. That's what you're going to find out."

"Yes, sir."

"Run away and we'll kill the darky for sure, and sell your horse, and then hunt you down."

"I promise not to run away."

"You're a liar, boy. Your promise don't mean nothing to me," he says with a sneer. "Only promise counts is this: If you run, my knife will find your back."

"Yes, sir."

We aren't but half a mile on the trail before the ground starts to slope away and the trees thin out, and the sky gets big and full of sunlight. At the bottom of the hill is a fine stone wall, straight as a schoolmarm's ruler, and beyond the stone wall, set like a jewel on the crown of a soft green hill, is a big house. An amazing house. A grand house made of stone and brick, with white pillars in the front and curtains in the windows and slate tiles on the roof and chimneys on every corner.

I'm thinking I'd give anything to live in a house like that, and be rich and happy and never have to worry about anything. And then Smelt yanks on the rope around my neck and says, "The best lie starts with the truth, boy. Tell 'em your name is Homer Figg and you're looking for your brother. Tell 'em your horse got stolen. Tell 'em you're hungry."

Smelt takes the rope off and shakes me, like he wants to make sure I'm paying attention. "You understand? Just get inside the house."

"Yes, sir."

"They'll likely take you straight to the kitchen. Brewster's cooks will fuss over a skinny runt like you, and want to fatten you up with biscuits and butter and honey. Sound good?"

"Yes, sir." It does sound good.

"Women who work in the kitchen will know everything that's going on in the house, and in the mines, too. All you have to do is keep your eyes and ears open."

"Yes, sir."

"After supper you make an excuse and go out to the privy. I'll be waiting."

I start to say "yes, sir," but he puts his finger on my lips and says, "Ssshh. Don't lie to me. I know what you're thinking. You're thinking how to get around old Smelt. Thinking how to sell me for butter and biscuits. All you have to know is this: If you don't come to old Smelt, old Smelt will come to you."

Then he lets me go.

8

PANCAKES
IN HEAVEN

THE HOUSE ON THE HILL gets bigger and bigger the closer I get. There are puffy white clouds reflected in the windows and the clouds are moving against the sky, and that makes it look like the whole house is moving, too. It's like I can feel the earth turning and have to be careful where to put my feet. The whole thing makes me so dizzy that the gentle green hill seems to get steeper and steeper and finally it tips up and I'm facedown in the grass.

Fainted from lack of food. All that talk about biscuits and butter and honey, it must have reminded my stomach that it hasn't had food since I wolfed down the slops intended for Squint's hogs, and started the whole terrible business of Harold getting sold to the army.

Soft, soft grass. Better than a pillow. Makes me forget I'm hungry, makes me forget everything.

Next thing I'm floating. No, not floating, I'm being carried, and there are gentle murmuring voices that sound like running water, and then I'm in a warm place and somebody is holding a cup to my lips and telling me to drink.

"Just a small sip," the voice says, and for a moment I think it's our Dear Mother and then I wake up and see big gray eyes studying me. Big gray eyes and rosy red cheeks and a helmet of fine white hair. "Turkey broth," she says. "Good for what ails you."

The lady with the gray eyes helps me sit up. She holds the cup while I sip the broth. Nothing ever tasted so good or made me feel so warm and safe and alive.

"Do you know where you are?" she asks.

"Big house," I say.

"The Brewster house," she explains. "I'm Mrs. Bean."

"Brewster bean," my tongue says.

"I'm the cook hereabouts," she gently explains, "and when they find a starving boy in the front yard, it's only natural they bring him to me."

Mrs. Bean takes the empty cup and says there's more where that came from, when I'm ready. She folds her plump arms and looks at me kind of sideways, as if trying to see inside my head. "Are you simple, dear? Or is it hunger makes you ramble?"

I take a deep breath and try to clear my head. Then I tell her who I am, like Smelt suggested, and that I'm looking for my brother, and that my horse got stolen, and leave out where I come from exactly, so nobody can send for Squinton Leach.

Seems like Mrs. Bean believes most of it because she starts nodding and saying, "Oh dear, oh dear," and I decide it's time to shed a tear or two for my lost brother, to really make her believe me, and the next thing I know she's hugging me and patting my head and promising that Mr. Brewster will find Harold.

"When Jebediah Brewster sets his mind to a thing, watch out!" she declares, dusting at her white apron. "Mr. Brewster will be back later, and you'll tell him what you told me. Orphan boy searching for his brother. That will get his attention."

Meantime Mrs. Bean makes it her mission to fill my belly. She asks would I rather have a plate of meat and gravy, or pancakes and bacon, and I go for the pancakes. While the bacon is sizzling in the big iron fry pan, the kind our Dear Mother called a "spider," I sit next to the stove and watch, because Mrs. Bean, she's something to see, the way her plump hands fly around the room like pale white birds, bringing things out of cupboards and jars and larder boxes.

"Can't help notice you lack shoes," she says, stirring flour into a blue mixing bowl. "Did you lose them along the way?"

Figure there's been enough truth for one day, so I say, "Yes, ma'am. Lovely pair of boots, made from the skin of a timber rattler."

"A rattlesnake! Oh my!"

"Yes, ma'am. Snake had me cornered when Harold wrassled it to death. Snake tried to spit in his eyes and blind him, but Harold was too quick. Broke its neck with one flick of his wrist."

"Amazing," she says. "A snake with a neck."

"Must have been thirty foot long."

Mrs. Bean nods. A little puff of flour comes up from the bowl. "And then your brother skinned the snake and made you boots, is that what you're telling me?"

I thought about that, and decided modification was in order. "Not exactly. Fact is, Harold did skin the beast, but I made the boots myself. Had a matching belt, too. They took everything."

"The thieves who stole your horse. What did you call that horse, now? King something or other."

"Prince Bob. Bob's a thoroughbred racehorse. Three years old and faster than a bee sting."

"Remarkable," says Mrs. Bean. "And where was it you said you came from?"

"Oh, up in the north," I say vaguely. "Little no-account place."

"Yes, but it must have a name, mustn't it? Every place has a name, no matter how small."

"Smelt," I tell her in a moment of inspiration.

"Excuse me?"

"Smelt. That's what they call it. On account of the swamp nearby."

I'm congratulating myself for not calling it Stink. Stink would be too much to believe, but Smelt is subtle. Smelt is rarified.

"Never heard of Smelt," Mrs. Bean allows, fixing her calm gray eyes on me. "Thought I knew every village in the state of Maine, at least by name. But I've never heard of Smelt."

I almost say that Smelt had never heard of her, either, but think better of it. Nothing like the prospect of pancakes to make me smart-mouthed and sassy.

Mouth shut, I take the time to survey Mrs. Bean's magnificent kitchen. The room is bigger than Squint's whole house, with a fry stove and a bake stove and a full fireplace with a Dutch oven. Pantry has more canned goods than the general store in Pine Swamp, and there are three different slate sinks, one for washing dishes and one for rinsing vegetables, and one just for the heck of it, I guess. Loads of cupboards with glass fronts, copper pots of every size, rock-maple countertops, a butter urn Mrs. Bean says belongs in a museum. And drawers. There are big drawers and little drawers and bread drawers and knife drawers, and linen drawers, and drawers for extra things left over.

Mrs. Bean suggests I stop opening and closing the drawers and sit down to pancakes and bacon. She pulls out a chair and scoots me up to the kitchen table. There on a big white china plate is a pile of pancakes I only ever dreamed about, because Squint never gave us more than stale bread and sour molasses. Pancakes slathered in yellow butter. Steaming pancakes drowned in warm maple syrup.

Figure Smelt must have killed me for sure, and I've woke up in Heaven. Or maybe I'm still so hungry I can't think straight. Then I decide that good as the pancakes taste, this can't be Heaven because there aren't any clouds or golden harps or angels with whispery wings. And God would be there, too, wouldn't He, if this was really Heaven?

That's when he comes in from the parlor, dressed all in black. God Himself.

9

QUAKER
TALK

THE MAN WHO LOOKS LIKE God Himself is Jebediah Brewster, owner of the house. He's got a long, flowing white beard, piercing blue eyes, and a booming voice that rattles the china when he bellows, "Hello!" A voice that freezes my brain and makes it hard to answer simple questions like, "What be thy name, son?" and "Where be thy home?"

Quaker talk.

"The young scallywag calls himself Homer and says he's from a place called Smelt," says Mrs. Bean, weighing in. "The only truthful part of him is the part that's hungry."

"Smelt, hey? Very interesting," Mr. Brewster responds in his kindly way. "All God's children are from somewhere. The precise location matters not. Thee be welcome in this house, Homer, whoever thee be and whatever has brought thee here."

Mr. Brewster sits down at the table, adjusts his black

sleeves, and announces that he will have a glass of cold water, if Mrs. Bean will be so kind as to oblige. He thanks her, takes the glass in both hands, and drinks it in three long gulps. His big throat moves under his beard and you can hear the water going down, like it was leaking out of an old hand pump.

"The finest spring water," he announces, dabbing delicately at his beard with a linen napkin. "That's what drew me to this particular location. Clear, cold spring water, steeped in the best minerals. It keeps the guts healthy and purifies the blood. I intended to bottle it as an elixir, and sell it by the drop, but in digging out the spring we encountered gemstones, and that became my business. Just one of the Lord's many surprises."

Mr. Brewster then folds his long-fingered hands like he's praying, and studies me for a while. As if he's looking at my soul, if I got one, and finds it wanting. Makes me fit to fidget, being studied like that, but I manage to hold still. Because both of 'em are waiting for me to tell a lie, I can sense that much.

"Does thee know much about gemstones, Homer?" Mr. Brewster asks, sweet as can be.

Something in me wants to say my third cousin Curtis McTavit has been trading gems for his whole life, and recently come into possession of the world's largest ruby that he got off the widow of Blackbeard the pirate, but that the ruby is cursed. Ever since he got the ruby, poor

McTavit lives in fear. He's barricaded himself inside his own dungeon and believes that the ruby speaks to him in the ghostly voices of all it has cursed. Course I don't have a cousin named Curtis McTavit, or any cousin I'm aware of, and I clamp my jaw shut until the urge passes.

"He's gone quiet," Mrs. Bean observes suspiciously. "Maybe it was starving made him talk so."

Mr. Brewster takes a deep breath and nods to himself, as if satisfied. "Homer Figg," he announces. "Thee may be an innocent stranger or thee may be a spy sent by those who oppose us, but one thing is clear to me. God has a hand in this, and He would not have us turn away a hungry child."

Mrs. Bean smiles at me and shrugs. I get the idea that nothing Mr. Brewster does surprises her.

"Come along, son," he says, standing up, "and thee will be shown the secret of Brewster Mines."

"The boy needs a bath," Mrs. Bean points out. "I doubt he's had a bath this year. And maybe last year, too."

"After he surveys the mine," says Mr. Brewster, clamping his hand on my shoulder. "After he's seen our amazing mine thee can scrub him until he bleeds."

I'm hoping that's just more Quaker talk, but Mrs. Bean has a soapy kind of gleam in her eye. Before I have time to make plans for escape, Mr. Brewster is marching me out the door and into the long grass. We're going uphill, away from the big house, away from the warm kitchen, and the sky is so thin and cool and blue it makes me feel a little out of breath somehow.

Pretty soon we come to a path, worn into ruts by wagon wheels, and then to a set of rusty iron rails hammered into the hillside. We follow the rails. From around the bend comes the gentle murmur of flowing water, but sound must be tricky in these hills because I never do see the water.

All the while Mr. Brewster's big voice never stops booming and it comes to me that he couldn't keep a secret even if it killed him, because secrets are related to lies, and I doubt Mr. Brewster ever lied in his whole life. Which reminds me of my brother, Harold, who is probably halfway to the war by now, and worrying about that makes it hard to concentrate on all the things Mr. Brewster is saying about gemstones and mines, and why God has put us on earth, and how He tests us.

"So I searched for healing water and instead found the rainbow," he's saying. "Not a pot of gold exactly, but a vast deposit of tourmaline, which comes in all the colors of the rainbow."

Tourmaline. Sounds like a pirate name to me. Must be I got pirates on the brain for some reason. But Mr. Brewster explains that tourmaline is a gemstone used in costume jewelry. When polished it shines like diamonds or rubies or emeralds, depending on how it's cut.

"Tourmaline brought me great wealth," he says. "It did not bring me wisdom or show me the path. It was God who provided wisdom, and Frederick Douglass who showed me the path."

Before he can explain, we come upon the mine itself.

I've been expecting a proper tunnel cut into the side of the mountain, like I've seen in storybooks, but Mr. Brewster's mine is more like a big pit in the ground. We're looking down on some rusty tin roofs and a bunch of rickety-looking shacks where the miners work, prying hunks of rock from the ground and cutting out the raw gemstone. Except there are no miners working, there's no one at all.

Mr. Brewster guides me down a narrow little pathway into the empty pit.

"This is the secret of Brewster Mines," he announces, quite happily. "We ceased production two years ago, when the war started."

"But why is that a secret?" I ask.

"Because the mine remains active," he says mysteriously. "It is convenient if the world assumes that the activity is related to mining. Folks think we provide lead and copper to the Union Army. That is not true, and I pray for forgiveness for letting it stand without correction. Because my untruthfulness is in the service of a greater good."

For once in my life I keep my mouth shut and wait for him to tell me whatever it is he wants to say. I assume he's going to confess there are fugitive slaves hid in the mines somewhere, like Smelt said, but I'm not supposed to know that, so I got to be ready to act surprised when it comes out.

Only it don't come out, not exactly.

Mr. Brewster drapes his long arm over my shoulders and

holds on, like he expects me to bolt any second. He lowers his big voice to a ragged whisper. "Ebenezer Smelt is well-known in these parts," he confides. "Mr. Smelt is often found in the company of William Mullins, better known as 'Stink.' I mention this because thee told Mrs. Bean thee hailed from a place called Smelt. To my knowledge, no such place exists. So I must assume thee are in league with the murderous Mr. Smelt and his evil associate."

I started out keeping my mouth shut on purpose, but Jebediah Brewster has knocked the words right out of me.

10

WHEN THE RIVER
CRIES LIKE A BABY

HAROLD READ ME A STORY once about a man who could see into your mind. Think of a number and he'd pull it out of a deck of cards. Man could tell what you were thinking before you thought it. He knew your aunt Mildred's birthday, and how many horses your brother owned, and if you preferred rhubarb to apple pie. At the end he saw things that got him tarred and feathered and run out of town on a rail, and that was the best part of the story.

I'm wondering if Jebediah Brewster has that same power to read minds. Doesn't seem possible he'd figure everything out because of one measly word.

Turns out it wasn't only the word *Smelt*, it was seeing the man himself.

"Mr. Smelt has been following us," Brewster explains softly, his hard blue eyes lifted to the hills around us. "Thinks he's being clever, but the good Lord gave me the eyes of an eagle. That isn't a dirty old weasel, that's Ebenezer Smelt, scuttling among the rocks. He's the color of dirt, but I see him, indeed I do."

"He made me do it," I manage to say. "Made me come here on a rotten lie."

Mr. Brewster and Mrs. Bean have been so good and decent it makes me want to cry, having to admit that I've been sent to betray them.

"Maybe he did and maybe he didn't," Mr. Brewster says, not unkindly. "Makes no difference. Our strategy remains the same. Let them watch us, Smelt and his confederates. See what it gets them, doing the Devil's work."

"They got a darky man," I tell him, eager to make up for all my falsehoods. "I think they mean to kill him, or sell him for a slave."

Brewster glances at me sort of sideways, his eyes never straying long from the hills. " 'Darky' is not a proper word," he says, very stern. "If a man has dark skin, say that he is colored, or that he is African. Or better yet, do not refer to his complexion. Does the Lord care if we be pink or brown? I assure thee, He does not."

"They put a sack on his head," I tell him. "The colored man."

"That would be Mr. Samuel Reed, the conductor," says Brewster, squinting into the distance. "He has been leading a group of slaves to freedom and was abducted two days ago. We've been on the lookout ever since."

I figure by conductor he means the colored man works

on a train, collecting tickets, but Mr. Brewster is talking about the Underground Railroad, which is a different thing. He explains there aren't any actual trains on the Underground Railroad, and no rails to speak of. But they do have conductors, who guide fugitive slaves from station to station. Each "station" being a house or a hiding place. Could be a root cellar or a shed or a mine, anywhere they can hide fugitives on their way north to Canada, where slavery has been outlawed.

"Thousands have come this way," he explains. "They are given safety at this station and many others like it. Men like Samuel Reed risk their own freedom so that others may be free. And men like Mullins and Smelt are always waiting in the shadows, eager to betray them for a few pieces of silver. The evil that men do for money continues to astound me. Are thee kin to such men, Homer Figg? Speak the truth, for I shall know if thee lie."

I decide that lying to Jebediah Brewster is like lying to God — you can't fool either one — so I tell him about coming upon Stink and Smelt in the woods. How they stole Bob the horse and took me prisoner, and how Smelt will be waiting for me when night comes, and that he will want to know where the fugitives have been hid.

Mr. Brewster nods. "It's as I suspected. Come along, Homer. Back to the house, as if we are not aware that Mr. Smelt is watching us. This evening after supper thee wilt report to him, as instructed."

"What should I tell him?" I ask. Mr. Brewster's smile is as hard and cold as a diamond gemstone. "Tell him the truth," he says. "The truth shall set thee free."

———

NIGHT NEVER TOOK SO LONG to come. It's like someone nailed the sun in the sky just to torment me. Because the last thing in the world I want to do is come face-to-face with Ebenezer Smelt. He might try to snatch me away, and even though Mr. Brewster says to tell him the truth, I'm afraid of what he'll do with the truth, because the real truth is I don't know what's going to happen when night finally gets here.

Mr. Brewster is as calm as some old white mountain waiting for the wind to wear it down. There's no rush about him. He waits like waiting is all he ever wanted to do.

"I was raised among the Society of Friends, the people thee call Quakers," he says, staring at me like a great bearded barn owl.

We're on the side porch, facing the rolling hills to the west, and every shadow looks like someone coming to steal me away. In the big warm kitchen Mrs. Bean is cooking supper. The smell of beef and potatoes wafting out to the porch makes my throat feel thick, like it's hard to swallow. Like I still have a few fat lies stuck in my throat.

"The Friends believe no man may be enslaved by another," Mr. Brewster continues, very stern. "We also believe no man has the right to kill another, even in war, no matter how just the war. Forbidden from the battlefield, I must find another path toward righteousness. Such a place is here," he says, thumping his rocking chair with his fist.

Jebediah Brewster stands up tall as the world and takes hold of my hand.

"Come along, Homer Figg. There's a sight thee must see."

He takes me to the basement door. Figure he's going to lock me up like Squint and throw away the key, except there are no locks on the doors in the Brewster house.

"Be not afraid," he says. "No harm will come to thee."

He lights a glowing lantern and throws open the basement door. From below comes the light of other lanterns and a gentle murmur that sounds like a deep river.

A deep river that cries like a baby.

11

THE WEASEL COMES
A-CALLING

THERE'S A WHOLE OTHER WORLD in Mr. Brewster's basement. Must be twenty people hiding down there, and two babies wrapped in blankets. Two or three families, all on the run, looking to find a new life. On the run, all the way from Maryland, with slave catchers dogging their trail. The fugitives look thin and hungry and scared. They jump at every sound from above. The squeak of the floor when Mrs. Bean walks across the kitchen, a window rattling in the wind, the sad cooing of a mourning dove up in the eaves—every noise makes them nervous and fearful.

Mr. Brewster says that fear is something slaves carry with them, and they won't be rid of it until they're safe across the border in Canada, with nobody to snatch them back. Some of these folks have escaped more than once, only to be seized by slave catchers and taken back. Makes it worse for this particular group because their brave conductor, Samuel

Reed, vanished into thin air. They figure if it can happen to him, it can happen to them.

If Stink and Smelt have their way, it will.

"All I do is offer shelter for a night or two," Mr. Brewster explains. "The real work, the dangerous work, is done by the likes of Mr. Reed."

The basement is fixed up real nice, with rugs on the floor and rows of sturdy bunks, and plenty of food, and special baffles to keep the lantern light from shining out the basement windows. It's way better than the barn where me and Harold lived. But no matter how nice Mr. Brewster made the place, it's still a kind of dungeon, even if there are no padlocks or chains. You can feel it in the air, the people wanting to get out, to be free of this place, or any place where they've got to be afraid.

"I would have these poor folk in my own house, as honored guests, but there are many who would burn us out if we did so," Mr. Brewster says, bringing me up out of the basement. "Burn us to the ground they would! Thee think runaway slaves are fearful? Their fear is nothing to the fear the white man has of the black. Abolitionists who preach against slavery will not let colored worshippers sit with whites in their churches. They think it unclean that light and dark should mix."

"How will they get to where they're going?" I ask.

"Same way they got here," he says. "On foot and in wagons. But mostly on foot. With slave catchers lurking, they

must travel at night, under c
on cloudy or moonless nigh
example."

He doesn't say so, exactly, b
be on the move tonight.

"What should I do?" I ask h

Mr. Brewster sets me down
Bean has put out steaming plate
ered in gravy.

"Thee must do whatever is tr
for me to force a thing upon th
as I believe."

I never had such a plate of foo
much for plates, for that matte
basement has killed my appetite
dren and babies, all running fr
them up, and buy them and sel
thinking how much I hated it w
us up, or whipped us with his b
army like he was something Squ

"Get a gun," I urge Mr. Brew

He shakes his great white hea
sworn to peace."

"Mrs. Bean," I say. "Tell him t

Mrs. Bean chuckles and give
up on that years ago," she says.
beliefs."

" If yo
plea ding
He si
"Th ee m
It a ll bo
life, to d
" Wh
" It m
hou se.
hur gry.
thi ng. S
som ethi
" Thi
gra vy la
" I kn
boy s are
ow n sla
" If y
be gging
" The
I sha
cra zy, a
pla gues
fat her,
bei ng s
the que
be tter

I won't get a gun, then tell me what to do," I ask,

hs so deep it   almost makes the windows rattle.
ıst decide," he says again. "But I will say this much.
ls down to this: A person has only two options in
 something or   to do nothing."
t's that supposed to mean?"
ans that if thee do nothing, thee may stay in this
hee will be safe and cared for and will never go
Mrs. Bean will see to that. Or thee can do some-
mething to help Mr. Smelt and his confederates, or
ıg to help those who have escaped their chains."
isn't fair," Mrs. Bean admonishes him, shaking her
dle. "He's just a boy, and a scrawny one at that!"
ow," says Mr.   Brewster, sounding regretful. "But
fighting this cruel war. Boys are enslaved, and boys
es. None may   escape. All must decide."
ou won't get   a gun then give me one," I ask,

,

e are no guns   in this house. Not for thy purpose."
ke my head. Comes to me that Jebediah Brewster is
ıd that's like God Himself being crazy. As crazy as
and pestilence, as crazy as the tree that fell on my
nd my Dear Mother dying so young, and Squint
 mean. I can't   stand another minute of this, with all
;tions in my head, trying to decide things that are
ft to God and   Mr. Brewster.

"Where are you going?" Mrs. Bean calls out when I get up from the table. "What are you going to do?"

But I'm running out the door without an answer. Running into the sooty blue darkness where Smelt is waiting. Smelt with his knife and probably a gun, too. And I've got no idea what to do, no idea at all.

Except I know one thing. I can't do nothing. Nothing is not an option.

12

THE DOOR
IN THE DIRT

BREWSTER'S PRIVY LOOKS better cared for than Squint's whole house and is nearly as big. It's got fancy wood trim, all painted neat and white, and a half moon cut in the door. Very civilized, and way better than the cow ditch me and Harold used when we had to do our business out behind the barn.

I'm most ways to the privy door when a dirt-colored hand clamps over my mouth and yanks me into the shadows behind the building.

Smelt with his knife, like I figured.

"Evening, boy," he whispers, his nasty little eyes flicking to the big house. "If you try and scream I'll wring your neck and drop your body into the cesspit. Nod if you understand."

I nod. Smelt grins, showing me his tooth.

"Fatten you up, did they? Fuss over you some? Hope you enjoyed it, boy. Hope you paid attention. 'Cause if you can't tell me where they hid them fugitives, this world's got no more use for Homer Figg. You might's well jump in that cesspit and save me the trouble."

My brain has been racing since I run from the house, trying to find a lie that will save me and the runaway slaves and Mr. Brewster, too. Comes to me in that very moment, with Smelt jabbing the point of his knife in my ribs, looking for a soft spot. Don't know if the lie is powerful enough to work, but it's the only one I have at the moment.

"Gemstones!" I exclaim. "Tourmaline!"

"Hush your voice, boy," he hisses.

"In the mine," I tell him. "They're hiding in the old tourmaline mine."

That filthy hand of his starts squeezing on my neck. "The mine? Who told you, the cook or the old man?"

"Showed me," I say, gasping as his hand tightens.

"You saying he took you up to the mine and showed you where he's got the slaves hid? You expect me to believe that?"

The part of the lie I'm counting on is that Smelt doesn't know he was spotted shadowing me and Jebediah Brewster to the mines. Best kind of lie has some truth in it, just like Smelt said. Used to drive my brother, Harold, crazy when I'd tell folks our Dear Father was killed by a tree that measured a mile high from roots to top. The tree was real but the mile wasn't, and Harold said that made it worse, telling a lie that was partway true.

I can see in Smelt's eyes that he's trying to catch me lying but hasn't so far, because he knows Mr. Brewster really did show me the mine.

"I been all over that site," Smelt says, puzzling it out. "Didn't see no fugitive slaves, nor any place to hide them."

"Old shed with a rusty tin roof," I tell him, making it up as I go along. "There's a secret passage in the shed."

"Nothing in that shed but rocks and dirt," he says suspiciously.

"Under the dirt," I tell him. "There's a door under the dirt. Mr. Brewster wouldn't let me go down there, but he lifted the door up enough with his foot so I could see the ladder down."

"Hole in the dirt don't mean nothing," he says. "It's a mine, there's lots of holes in the dirt."

"Heard a baby crying," I tell him.

That gets his attention. Probably he knows the fugitives have a child or two. "Baby cryin', you say?"

"Yes, sir."

He presses the knife harder. Another twitch and he'll be drawing blood. "Tell me the truth now. Why'd a man like Jebediah Brewster show you where he's hid them fugitives? Why'd he trust a lyin' boy like you?"

"Said it was up to me, whether I wanted to help or run away."

Smelt makes a face, nods to himself. "Sounds like that Quaker fool."

"So now you know, right?"

"Maybe I do and maybe I don't."

"I did what you wanted. Give me back my horse."

That makes him laugh. "It's my horse now, for sparin' your worthless life."

"You promised to let me go," I insist. "I've got to find my brother before he gets to the war."

In the dark he looks like a jack-o'-lantern with one snaggle tooth, grinning me for a fool. "That wasn't the deal. The deal was, do like I say and I might let you live. It's still a 'might,' boy. Show me this door in the dirt and then we'll see who is lying and who is dying."

Then he stuffs a rag in my mouth, whips a rope around my wrists, and drags me off into the night.

———

WHEN I WAS LITTLE, and we first went to live with our uncle Squinton Leach, the thing I was most scared of, other than the dark, was my brother, Harold, disappearing. Our father was gone and our Dear Mother, too, and it seemed like my big brother would be next and then I'd be all alone in the world. I'd wake up crying and afraid, and to soothe me Harold told stories about pirates and Indians. The pirates and Indians wanted to get us, but couldn't, no matter how hard they tried. Harold always made me the one who saved us. I'd trick the pirates and we'd get away. Or I'd show him how to hide from the Indians, and he'd tell me how clever and brave I was, only it was him making up the story, not me.

Harold never believed in pirates, not real pirates, and the only Indians left in Pine Swamp worked for the timber company, felling trees. It was only made-up stories to make me feel safe. We never had a story about someone like Ebenezer Smelt because we never knew a man that bad really existed. A man that'll hunt innocent people like animals and drag a boy through the dark of night and threaten to kill him.

Some things are worse than the worst kind of nightmare, and it turns out the only thing worse than Ebenezer Smelt is his partner, Stink Mullins, who's waiting for us in the woods.

The moment we get there Stink grabs the rope, throws me to the ground, and kicks the air out of me.

"You was thinkin' something bad," he says, satisfied. "That'll teach you." Then he grabs the rag from my mouth and dabs at his empty eye socket. Lucky for me he decides to keep the rag, and jams it in his pocket.

"Where they hid?" he asks Smelt. "The boy find out?"

"Says they're at the mine, in a secret tunnel."

"You believe him, do you?"

"I don't believe nothing till I see it with my own eyes. Where's Festus?"

"In the lean-to, trussed up like a turkey," Stink says with a chuckle. "That darky is too scared to move, let alone get himself free."

I don't know why they call Samuel Reed, the conductor, Festus. I figure he's got about as much chance of seeing the sunrise as I do, once they figure out I'm lying about the mine. Unless I can come up with a better lie, one that will set us both free.

"They on the move tonight?" Stink asks, prodding at me with his boot.

Best I can do is nod. That's enough to get us up and moving again. There's no moon in the sky, and only a few dim stars showing through the clouds, but the two men know where they're going. Before long we're on the trail up to the mine, following the wagon ruts. The dark feels heavy, like a thick blanket that won't let you breathe, and the ground is hard and sharp under my feet.

Suddenly Smelt holds up his hand and stops us. "You hear that?"

Pebbles skitter down from the hills around us.

"Ground is always moving here," says Stink. "All that scavenge from the mine."

"Something's out there," Smelt complains. "Something alive."

"Raccoon or a skunk," says Stink with a laugh. "What you afraid of?"

"Nothin'."

"Afraid of an old Quaker man that won't lift a hand to defend himself? 'Fraid of a bunch of scared-to-death darkies?"

"Shut up."

The strange thing of it is, the closer we get to the mine, the calmer I feel. Doesn't make sense, because I still don't know what to say when they find there's no door in the dirt. Maybe the strange calm feeling is what happens when a man stands up for the firing squad, or climbs the gallows to be hung. Like you're calm because the waiting part is almost over, and you're tired of being afraid.

Only difference, it's so dark I won't need a blindfold.

We come at last to the old tin shed, in a place so empty even the ghosts have gone away.

Stink pulls me up short on the rope. He smells worse than the cesspit. Worse than rotten eggs, or a dead cat. "No sense waiting," he says to Smelt, unsheathing his knife. "The slaves are here or they ain't. Either way, Homer Figg has outlived his usefulness."

I'm trying to decide should I close my eyes or not, when all of a sudden the darkness moves and takes the shape of a man.

Samuel Reed, freed from his bonds, is swinging a six-foot iron bar like it's a baseball bat, and Stink Mullins is a cheap home run.

13

A Wagonload
of Hope

THE FIRST SWING DROPS Stink like a bag of smelly potatoes. He's out cold, not moving.

If I was Ebenezer Smelt and saw what happened to my
partner, I'd hightail it and run for my life, but old Smelt
decides to stand his ground.

"Put down that weapon!" he screams. "You're my lawful
prisoner!"

Smelt drops into a fighting crouch, jabbing away with
his big blade, looking for an opening, but he can't get close
enough to Samuel Reed to poke him with the knife.

Reed doesn't say a word. He just swings that heavy iron
bar like it was a twig. The hiss of it cutting the air sounds
like a cold steel snake eager to strike.

"You'll hang for this!" Smelt promises, but he's starting
to sound afraid.

Samuel Reed takes careful aim, and when Smelt gets too
close, the iron bar smacks his hand and his knife goes flying
into the dark.

Smelt scrambles after it, cursing, and the iron bar catches him hard in the butt, knocking him down flat. When he tries to sit up — big mistake — Mr. Reed whomps him on the head and his eyes roll white and he falls back unconscious.

Then a strange thing happens. Samuel Reed drops the iron bar like it's burning his hands and covers his eyes and starts to weep.

"But you won," I tell him, confused. "You got 'em good!"

Mr. Reed takes a deep breath and stops sobbing. "I was a dead man," he says in a husky voice. "Dead man has nothin' to lose, nothin' to be feared of. Now I'm back among the living and scared to death about what happens next. Does that make sense?"

Only thing makes sense is taking care of those two villains before they wake up and try to kill us. Reed helps me get the rope off my wrists and we use it to lash Stink and Smelt together, hands behind their backs. Seems like Samuel Reed has lost all his strength and it's up to me to make sure the knots are good and tight.

When we're done we start the long walk back to Mr. Brewster's house. Samuel Reed has started to limp from his efforts, and has to lean on me for support.

"Used up everything I had," he explains, panting. "No food for three days, precious little water."

"How'd you manage to get free?" I ask him.

"Jebediah found me in the woods," he says. "You told him

about me, and he had a good notion of where to look. Knows these lands like the back of his hand, does Jebediah."

"Why'd you follow us here to this old mine?" I want to know. "Why not take the fugitives and go?"

Reed shrugs. "That's what I first thought to do. Get away quick as I could. But then I thought about how these two men would follow us, and how you'd helped me out there in the woods."

"I didn't do much," I say.

"It was enough," says Reed, patting the top of my head. "They'd have killed me if you hadn't convinced them I was worth more alive."

"Then we're even, 'cause you saved my life, too. I was a goner for sure."

As we walk along, following the wagon ruts in the dark of a moonless night, Mr. Reed starts to recover a little of his strength. He wipes the last tears from his eyes and says it will be a busy night, there is still much to do.

"How long will it take for the fugitives to get away?" I ask.

"We leave tonight," Mr. Reed explains. "Two or three days to reach the border, if the weather holds."

"And you will lead them."

"That's what I do," he says.

THE WARM GLOW OF THE LANTERN in the Brewster house guides us, and when we finally limp into the yard, holding each other up, there are two wagons in the drive-way, each with a team of horses snorting and pawing the ground, as if eager to get moving. The fugitives who had been hiding in the basement are climbing into the wag-ons, carrying their few belongings and huddling together. I never seen such a mournful group — you'd think they was on their way to a funeral instead of freedom.

Mrs. Bean is the first to see us coming out of the darkness.

"There they are!" she cries out. "Alive! Both alive!"

The fugitives swarm from the wagons, whooping out with joy. They grab hold of Samuel Reed and clap him on the back and then lift him up and carry him to the wagons. Everybody crying and laughing at the same time, joyous to have their hero back among the living. Amazing how fast the funeral turns into a welcome-home party, and how Mr. Reed seems to draw even more strength from his friends, until he looks as strong as when he was swinging that iron bar.

"Hush now!" he orders them, grinning. "You'll wake the whole county. Into the wagons, quickly, quickly. Make haste! We must be miles from here before dawn."

A few minutes later they're all back in the wagons, ready to go. All those dark faces full of new hope. Even the babies have stopped crying and burble happily in their mothers' arms.

Samuel Reed climbs up into the driver's seat of the first wagon and takes the reins.

Jebediah Brewster steps forward, holding a lantern. He shakes Mr. Reed's hand and says, "Godspeed and God bless. I'll await word that thee are safe across the border before releasing Mr. Smelt and his associate."

Mr. Reed snaps the reins and the wagons rumble out of the long drive and slowly melt away into the night.

Seems like this would be a good time for me to slip away, too, see if I can locate Bob the horse and be on my way. Every minute I was here is a minute closer to the war for my big brother, Harold. But when I turn to go, Mrs. Bean sweeps me up in her plump arms and hugs me and smothers my face with icky kisses.

"Never thought a boy could be good and a liar, too. But you are," she says. "You are."

14

THE HUNGRY
MOUSE

THERE MUST BE SOMETHING about a goose-down mattress that makes you dream of things that can't be true. Like our parents are still alive in our little house, and my father is smoking his long clay pipe by the fire, and our Dear Mother is reading me and Harold a story from a book she holds in her lap. The story is about an Indian scout and his adventures in the deep forests. There's another story about a funny little man who goes to sleep for a hundred years in a cave, or maybe that's a story Harold told me later, because the dream is fading and I can't hold it, no matter how hard I try.

Morning at Jebediah Brewster's house. The sun comes in like warm honey, and I can smell whatever Mrs. Bean is cooking for breakfast. Something with baked apples and brown sugar and cinnamon.

I hate to get out of bed—I never been in anything so soft or cozy. Makes me want to fall back asleep and find that dream where my parents are still alive and Harold is safe and wars are in storybooks from a long time ago.

I could do it, too. Mr. Brewster wants me to stay. He says a twelve-year-old boy has no business chasing an army on the way to war, and I can stay here and help him with the Underground Railroad. He says that getting beat by a colored man is so humiliating Smelt and Stink will never bother us again, and there are still wagonloads of fugitives who need help.

Part of me really wants to do it. Wants to forget about my brother and live in the lap of luxury, and get fat on pancakes and apple pie and pork cutlets and pan-fried chicken and ginger cookies with sugar on top. Maybe go back to Pine Swamp one day, riding in a fine carriage and dressed like a gentleman. Show old Squint what became of that ragged boy he kept in the barn like an animal.

But no matter how hard I try, I can't forget my brother Harold, marching to war on his bare feet, without even a real gun. Sleeping on the cold ground without enough to eat, nor clean water to drink, and sickness everywhere. He's so brave and honorable and careless of himself that he'll get killed for sure, and it will be my fault for not trying hard enough to save him.

Mrs. Bean is stuffing me with scrambled eggs and fried potatoes and apple crisp when Mr. Brewster looks into the kitchen and says, "Good morning, Homer. Has thee decided?"

"Let the boy have his breakfast in peace," says Mrs. Bean, shaking a spatula in his direction.

"Thee is right, of course. My apologies," he says, retreating.

"No," I call out. "Wait."

Mr. Brewster comes into the kitchen, looking at me kindly, but sort of worried. Mrs. Bean just shakes her head and sighs, and then pretends to fuss at the stove.

"My brother is my whole family," I tell him. "They tricked him and sold him like they sell a slave."

"And thee means to find thy brother, no matter what?"

"Yes, sir. I must."

"How will thee find him?" Mr. Brewster wants to know.

"First I'll try and locate Bob the horse."

Mr. Brewster looks thoughtful. "Assuming thee locates this horse, then what?"

I've got it all planned, except for all the nagging details. "Ride south until I find the army," I tell him.

"That's it?" he says doubtfully. "Ride south and hope for the best?"

"I can follow south," I assure him. "Don't need a compass to follow south, if you know where the sun rises and where it goes down."

"And if I said thee were but a child, and must stay here under my guardianship?"

Lying to Jebediah Brewster doesn't work, so I tell him the truth. "I'm grateful for your kindness, but I'll run away. I must."

He nods his great white head, like he already knew the answer. "The old horse is in the stable. It has been curried and watered, and given hay and oats."

Bob the horse is alive! Good old Bob! I can't wait to see him, and jump up from the table before the apple crisp is gone.

"Sit thee down," Mr. Brewster says, very stern. "Finish the food that has been blessed in this house."

"Yes, sir," I say, slumping back into the chair. "But Bob, he—"

"The horse will keep. Indeed, he will keep very well while thee journey by train and steamship to New York."

"Steamship?" I ask, puzzled. "New York?"

Mr. Brewster looks at Mrs. Bean, who is still fretting by the stove, pretending that she doesn't care what foolishness we're talking about. "I have made certain inquiries," he says, sounding very grave and serious. "Men recently enlisted in the state of Maine will stop in New York before joining up with the Union Army. It's likely thy brother will be among them, and that he will have been transported on a troop train or possibly by steamship. Certainly it is much too far to travel by horse."

Suddenly I get a picture in my mind of Harold on a train with hundreds of other soldiers. He's never been on a train before. Will he be scared or excited? Likely both, knowing

Harold. Here I'd been thinking he'd have to march all the way to the war, but trains make more sense, if the whole point is getting men to where the shooting starts as quick as possible.

"Does it cost a lot to get there?" I ask. "I could sell you Bob. He's a good old horse."

Mr. Brewster smiles. "The animal is certainly old, I'll grant thee that much. Never mind the cost of the journey, I'll provide it gladly. And if I was not so urgently occupied here, I would accompany thee myself. But I dare not leave. Ebenezer Smelt may be gone, but there are like-minded men who will take his place."

"I'll be fine," I say grandly. "Don't you worry about Homer Figg!"

That makes Mrs. Bean roll her eyes, but at least she's smiling again.

"No," says Mr. Brewster. "I cannot in good conscience let thee proceed alone. I have arranged to have a young Methodist clergyman act as thy guardian. He will be supplied with sufficient funds to buy thy brother out of enlistment."

It all sounds good to me. Better than good, because I get to see what a train looks like, and ride a steamship, and Harold gets out of the army. Then we'll both come back to live with Mr. Brewster, and I'm pretty sure he won't make us sleep in the barn.

Sitting in that warm and wonderful kitchen, it seems

like all my dreams are about to come true. Of course if I'd known what was going to happen, I'd have taken Bob the horse, or my own two feet—anything but get on that train.

Trouble is, I had no more sense than a hungry mouse. I saw the cheese and never paid attention to the trap. Trap by the name of Willow.

The Reverend Webster B. Willow.

15

TRAIN
TO GLORY

SOON AFTER BREAKFAST my new guardian shuffles into
the drawing room, walking like he's got something sticky
on his boots that makes it hard to lift his feet from the
floor. He's tall and thin, with narrow shoulders not much
wider than his head, and long skinny arms that shoot past
his frayed cuffs. He's wearing an old black frock coat, short
at the waist, and trousers that shine at the knees, and a
crooked stovepipe hat that bumps against the door frame
as he enters the room.

"Pardon me, sirs!" he exclaims, blushing. "A thousand
apologies! Oh dear, oh dear!"

Mr. Webster B. Willow don't look much older than my
brother, Harold. The fine blond hair on his narrow chin
hasn't decided if it wants to be a beard, and his eyes are so
close together it looks like he's studying his nose or trying
to see around it. Mostly he seems to be upset about forget-

ting to take off his hat like a gentleman does when entering a house, and he looks like he wants to leave the room and try again.

"Never mind the hat, Webster," says Mr. Brewster impatiently. "The hat is of no consequence. Come in, come in. I want thee to meet Homer Figg. He will be in thy charge."

"Splendid, wonderful, how do you do, sir," he says, grabbing my hand and shaking it without actually looking at me. "Wonderful opportunity! Splendid!"

He fidgets nervously with his dented hat while Mr. Brewster explains that we shall journey by train to Portland, and from there take an overnight steamship to New York.

"We can't be exactly sure where or when Homer's brother has been assigned," Mr. Brewster says. "It is likely that all the new recruits will be sent to encampments in New York or New Jersey and from there dispatched to the field of battle. Is that clear?"

"Field of battle, yes," says Mr. Willow.

"Thee will have to make inquiries once thee has reached New York," Mr. Brewster says, focusing upon the young clergyman. "I will provide thee with letters of introduction to newspaper editors, should that be useful, and to the local elders of my church. But thee will have to use thine own ingenuity to accomplish this task, understood?"

"Ingenuity," says Mr. Willow. "Indeed."

"Thee must be clear in thy purpose, Webster, lest thee be mistaken for a spy."

The idea alarms Mr. Willow. "Spy? Spy? They hang spies, don't they?"

"Indeed they do," says Mr. Brewster gravely. "But thee will not be spying. Thee are simply inquiring as to the whereabouts of an underage soldier who was taken into the army on a ruse. Thee will secure his release by legal means."

Mr. Brewster makes it sound pretty easy. All we have to do is go someplace and ask some questions and my brother will be released from the army.

———

THE NEXT DAY, AFTER a long carriage ride to the station, me and Mr. Willow find ourselves in a Boston and Maine Railroad car, bound for Portland. While the locomotive sits at the station building up steam, we wait on seats made from varnished oak. Everybody is dressed up like they're on their way to church. Women with long starched dresses and bonnets tied under their chins, and men in black wool suits, storing their tall hats in a special rack above their heads, and a conductor in a fine uniform, collecting tickets.

"Steam up in ten minutes, ladies and gentlemen!" he calls out. "Steam up in ten! Take your seats! Take your seats, if you please!"

Mr. Willow is feeling a bit nervous and confides that he has never been to Portland, let alone New York. "Truth is, I have never been on a train and have never seen a steamship with my own eyes."

I tell him not to feel bad— until a few days ago I had never been anywhere but Pine Swamp, and once to Skowhegan for the state fair.

"How far is it to Portland?" I want to know.

Mr. Willow has no idea, so I ask the conductor. "Thirty-eight miles, station to station," he announces, sounding very pleased with himself. "Time of travel, approximately one and a half hours."

Almost forty miles and we'll be there in less than two hours! That's faster than a racehorse can run flat out, and a horse can't run but a few miles before it needs to rest. But when I try to discuss the subject of speed and horses and trains, which is really quite interesting, Mr. Willow says he feels faint.

"I am distinctly indisposed," he complains in a sickly voice. "I must be ill from the motion. Rail sickness, they call it."

"We're not moving yet, Mr. Willow," I point out.

He does look pale, but when the whistle blows and the train lurches forward Mr. Willow recovers some of his good spirits. Buildings and trees and telegraph poles begin to rush by the windows, and the wheels start ticking against the rails in a kind of pleasant, peaceful way. "Not so very bad," he says, looking pleasantly surprised. "Indeed not."

Now that he's feeling better Mr. Willow wants to talk about himself. He tells me all about the little school where he pursued his Bible studies, the prizes he won for quoting Scripture, and how he had the good fortune to meet Jebediah Brewster at an abolitionist rally, and how Mr. Brewster has taken him under his wing and is helping to find him a position. "I am not presently affiliated with any particular congregation," he confides. "I am open to possibilities. Indeed, indeed."

The way he talks, Mr. Willow believes that helping me rescue my brother is a kind of test, and if he passes, Mr. Brewster will find him a congregation.

"A great man has given me his trust and I shall not let him down," he announces, very solemn.

After a while Mr. Willow's voice kind of blends into the sound of the wheels clicking against the rails. It's amazing what goes by the windows on a train. Farms and fields and forests, and rows of wooden houses, and big brick mills. Like we're floating through a storybook and each turn in the track is a new page, and it's a story I never heard before so I don't know how it will end. Page after page, picture after picture, and always something new around the corner, and the chugging of the locomotive belching black smoke, making its own dark clouds against the sky, and the steam whistle sounding alive somehow, like the whole train is saying, *Here-I-am, make-way-chugga-chugga-woowoo! Here-I-am, make-way-chugga-chugga-woowoo!* and rocking me to sleep.

When I wake up we're in Portland, and that's where the trouble really starts.

16

FRANK T. NIBBLY, ENTIRELY AT YOUR SERVICE

AN OLD COBBLESTONE STREET leads to Portland Harbor, and everybody at the train station said we can't miss it, our feet will tell us when we get there, but miss it we do. Seems that Mr. Willow hasn't got no more sense of direction than a blind kitten, and won't stop to ask along the way because he's afraid of pickpockets and thieves.

"A great man has entrusted me with a sum of money," he mutters to himself, checking his pockets. "I dare not risk it."

I've got my eyes peeled for lowlifes, figuring a city like Portland might have its own versions of Smelt and Stink lurking about, but we don't run into anybody that fits the description. Matter of fact, no one seems to be paying us any mind as we wander through fine neighborhoods of big houses shaded by giant elms.

"Oh dear," says Mr. Willow. "I seem to have gotten turned around again. Didn't we pass that yellow house before?"

"Twice," I tell him. "We're heading uphill."

"Indeed we are," he says. "Are you averse to going uphill?"

"I expect the water part of the city will be downhill, Mr. Willow."

"Really?" he asks, as if shocked by the idea. "Extraordinary!"

"Let's go downhill for a while," I suggest. "See where it takes us."

Mr. Willow lets me tug him along by the sleeve and in a few minutes we get clear of the big elm trees and see the sparkling harbor laid out before us. The port is packed with ships of every size and shape. There are schooners and paddlewheel steamships and sloops and ferryboats and wherries and more kinds of vessels than I ever imagined, all crowded together along the waterfront like bees trying to feed at a hive.

"Oh my," says Mr. Willow, staring in wonder. "Oh my, oh my."

Now that we can see where we're headed and keep the busy harbor in sight, we're able to cut through the side streets and down the pretty hills until finally we find the promised cobblestones under our feet, and the big iron gates to the steamship lines dead ahead.

The cobblestones are mobbed with people in a hurry

to get somewhere. Fine people in fine clothes, and workmen in rags, and police and sailors. Boys no older than me are loading carts and smoking clay pipes and looking very superior.

"Look out! Make way!"

When a fast carriage comes through, rattling over the stones, we have to step quickly to the side or risk getting run down. That's how we happen to make the acquaintance of beautiful Kate Nibbly and her brother Frank.

In her rush to avoid the carriage and keep her skirts clear of the filthy street, Miss Nibbly somehow bumps into Mr. Willow and ends up sprawled in his long skinny arms.

"Dear me!" he exclaims, finding her there. "Oh my!"

"Thank you, kind sir," she says, fluttering a pair of soft gloves at his twitching nose. "You have saved me from ruining my dress."

Before Mr. Willow can answer, I hear another voice coming up quick behind us.

"Sister, are you okay? Have you been injured?"

That's her brother Frank, who looks to be about Mr. Willow's age, and dressed like a prosperous gentleman, with a finely tailored suit, a gold chain to hold his pocket watch, gleaming leather shoes, and a mustache that curls up at the ends. Once he realizes what has happened—that the skinny clergyman has saved his sister from falling down or worse—he can't thank Mr. Willow enough.

"My dear fellow," he exclaims, seizing Mr. Willow's

hand and shaking it. "Well done! Well done! Kate, have you thanked this brave gentleman?"

"Yes, brother," she says, sounding ever so sweet and meek. "I let him kiss my gloves."

Mr. Willow's face gets as red as a ripe tomato, but he seems very pleased with himself. Frank looks things over, a big smile on his face, and his friendly eyes glint with humor. "Kissed her gloves, did you? Why that's practically a proposal of marriage."

Mr. Willow commences to stutter and squeak like a tea kettle coming to boil, but Frank laughs and claps him on the back. "I jest, sir! A joke! And for being such a good sport, I must insist that you join us for a bite to eat."

"Oh no," says Mr. Willow, blushing some more. "Can't. Mustn't. We have a steamship to catch."

"Really? What ship, pray tell?"

"The *Orion*," says Mr. Willow. "Bound for New York."

Frank and his sister look at each other and burst out laughing. "Excuse me," says Frank when he gets his breath back. "No insult intended. But it seems we will be shipmates, for Kate and I have booked the same ship, for the same destination."

"Amazing," says Mr. Willow, his jaw dropping open in wonder.

"Not so very amazing," says Frank, easily slipping his arm in Mr. Willow's, and steering him toward the waterfront. "Half the folks on this street are heading for the steamships. But never mind, fate is fate, and now you really must join us for muffins and chocolate. The good ship *Orion* won't leave for two hours yet, so there's plenty of time to get acquainted."

"And who is this?" Kate asks, flicking her gloves on my head. "Your servant boy? Can't say he's doing much for you."

Something about the way she flicks those gloves, something about a very cool look in her beautiful gray eyes, something about Kate Nibbly just gets my goat. So I snatch the gloves from her hand—why's she carrying them instead of wearing them, anyhow?—and I drop them in the gutter.

Miss Nibbly stares at me in disbelief. I'm expecting her to get angry, but instead she sighs and says, "I take it you are no servant boy?"

"No, ma'am, I am Homer Figg, and Mr. Willow is my temporary guardian until we get to New York and find my brother, Harold, except it looks like I'll be guarding him—Mr. Willow, I mean. He's a nice man but he hasn't the sense God gave to a billy goat."

"Homer?" says Mr. Willow, momentarily distracted. "What's that you say?"

"Told her you were a clergyman, Mr. Willow."

"What an interesting boy," Kate says, retrieving her gloves. "I just know we're going to be great friends."

She smiles at me and then gives her brother a look, like

she wants him to pay attention to something important, and then Frank Nibbly suddenly grins and claps his hands together and says, "Homer Figg! Splendid! So you're the cause of this journey, are you?" He reaches out, shakes my hand before I can snatch it away. "I've forgotten my manners. Allow me to introduce myself. Frank T. Nibbly, attorney-at-law, justice of the peace, and entirely at your service."

Here's something I didn't know, but soon found out: When a lawyer shakes your hand and smiles with just his teeth, you best run for your life.

17

MESSAGE
FOR HOMER FIGG

LIVE IN A BARN AND YOU get used to having all kinds of creatures around. Horses and cows and pigs, and wild things like owls and mice and snakes. One time Harold and I watched a fat black snake swallow a little gray mouse. It was the most amazing thing because the mouse never moved or tried to get away. It was like the mouse knew it was snake food and didn't want to make trouble.

That's pretty much how Mr. Willow acts with the beautiful Kate Nibbly. His eyes even blink like mouse eyes and he shivers like a mouse whenever she says things like "Oh really, Webster? How simply fascinating!" or "What's your opinion, Webster, should I wear the pearl necklace or do you prefer the amber?"

Haven't known her five minutes and already she's Kate and he's Webster, and you'd think they've been sweethearts

for years. We're sitting in a little restaurant at the steamship terminal, eating butter muffins dipped in chocolate
and glasses of ice-cold milk. Miss Nibbly is busy making
Mr. Willow feel like he's the most important man who ever
lived, and her brother Frank is being ever so nice to me.

"You say your brother was sold into the army? Extraordinary. What a terrible injustice. The whole purpose of
the war is to end slavery, is it not?"

"I don't know what the purpose of the war is," I tell him,
talking around a mouthful of muffins. "I just don't want
Harold getting killed is all."

"Of course you don't," Frank says, sipping delicately at
his glass of milk. "The loyal brother. How touching. And
you say this enterprise, this urgent journey to free your
brother, is being financed by Jebediah Brewster, of the
famous Brewster Mines?"

I didn't say no such thing, but Mr. Willow did, blurt-
ing out all our private business the first time Miss Nibbly
asked. How Mr. Brewster is testing his character by sending
him as my guardian, and how he has letters of introduction
to very important people, and how he's been instructed to
purchase Harold's release, if it comes to that.

He does everything but show her the money entrusted
to him by Mr. Brewster, and that's only because I jump on
his shoe.

"Homer, what has gotten into you?" he asks, rubbing his
skinny foot.

"Time we got on the ship, Mr. Willow."

"There's no hurry," says Frank Nibbly, showing me his teeth. "No hurry at all."

But the other passengers are saying their good-byes and starting to board the steamship *Orion*, and the stewards are loading up the trunks and baggage, and clouds of smoke are coming out of the smokestack. Mr. Willow finally notices what's happening and jumps up like somebody stuck him with a darning needle.

"The boy is right!" he blurts. "We must go! Can't miss the ship!"

When Mr. Willow makes it clear we really do have to board, I figure that will be the end of it, because something tells me the Nibblys don't really have tickets for the steamship, but want to trick us into missing the boat so they can figure out how to fool Mr. Willow into giving them the money.

They're after the money. I know it and Frank knows it and Kate knows it. The only one who doesn't know what's really going on is poor Mr. Willow. I grab him by the cuff and drag him to the gangway, into the crowd of passengers who are boarding. He keeps looking back at Miss Nibbly and she keeps batting her eyelashes, but finally we're at the top of the gangway and a man is asking for our tickets.

"Tickets? Tickets?" says Mr. Willow, looking confused. He pats his pockets and my heart sinks, but then he finds the envelope and hands over the tickets and the man is shooing us aboard, telling us to make way for the other passengers.

My idea is to hurry along to the cabins, but Mr. Willow turns back to the rail, looking for Miss Nibbly in the crowd below.

Frank and Kate are nowhere to be seen.

"Where can she have gone?" Mr. Willow wants to know.

It's on my tongue to say they're off looking for another sucker, but the poor man looks so hurt I decide to keep my mouth shut.

———

If the cabins on the steamship *Orion* were any smaller they'd be cages, and me and Mr. Willow would be clucking like chickens. There's barely room to open the door, and the bunks are so short and narrow that Mr. Willow has to practically fold himself in half before he can lie down. It's not so bad for me—I mostly fit—and from the top bunk I can see out the little window. I lie there and watch the light fade from the sky until the stars come out.

We could walk the promenade deck, like most of the other passengers are doing, or visit the dining room, or maybe even explore the steam engines, or tour the wheel-house, but Mr. Willow doesn't want to leave the cabin. I never seen a man go lovesick before, but there's no doubt about what's wrong with Webster Willow. He's pining for Kate Nibbly. A few hours ago he never knew she existed, and now he can't live without her.

"You need to see a doctor," I advise. "Maybe get some pills, or some leeches to draw away the sick blood."

"Shut up, Homer."

"See? If you were feeling well, you'd never tell anyone to shut up. You're much too polite."

"Go away and leave me alone."

"Can't," I say from my perch on the top bunk. "You're my guardian. If I was to fall off the ship or jump into the boiler, Mr. Brewster would hold you responsible and you'd never get your own congregation."

"Jump off the ship for all I care," he says, his voice muffled by the pillow he's hugging to his face. "You never liked her," he wails. "It's all your fault!"

There's a bunch of things I could tell him, if only he'd listen. How it's as plain as the long, skinny nose on his face that Miss Nibbly doesn't really care about him, but only about the money. How one liar can always recognize another, and I right away recognized two of 'em in Frank and Kate Nibbly, from the moment she pretended to fall into Mr. Willow's arms. How some folks are just naturally decent and truthful like Harold and Mr. Willow, and others are always scheming and taking advantage.

I could tell him all these things, but Mr. Willow jams the pillow over his head and so I'm left talking to myself, and listening to the steady throb of the great steam engine, and feeling the steady *whoosh!* of water running by the hull, *whoosh! whoosh! whoosh!* like the ocean is telling me a story but I can't hear it until I'm sound asleep.

When the knock comes on the cabin door I wake up so fast I bump my head on the ceiling.

"Homer Figg! Message for Homer Figg!"

Mr. Willow is snoring like a sawmill, so it's up to me to jump down from the bunk and open the cabin door.

A ship's steward stands in the passageway. He's wearing a funny little hat that buckles under his chin, and a smart uniform with gold stripes running down his trousers, and tight little shoes polished like black mirrors, and clean white gloves on his elegant little hands. His little eyes are as cold as chips of black ice.

"Homer Figg?"

"Yes, sir, that's me."

"The captain has requested your presence," he announces, sounding very full of himself. "Follow me, please."

If the captain wants to see me I must have done something wrong, but I can't for the life of me think what that could be, since so far I've been in the cabin the whole trip, looking out for poor Mr. Willow. Still, when the captain of a steamship gives an order, you'd best comply, so I tuck in my shirt and follow the steward as he marches smartly through the dim passageway and out to the open deck, where the smell of salt and sea wakes me all the way up.

The steward gives me a stern look, then takes a thick brass key from his pocket and locks the passageway door behind us.

"Where's the captain?" I ask.

"In his cabin fast asleep," the steward says, pocketing the

key. He touches his hand to his little hat and then slips away into the darkness so fast I don't have time to follow.

It comes to me the captain never wanted to see me — probably he's never even heard of Homer Figg — and that someone has paid the steward to get me out of the cabin and lock the door behind me.

I run along the deck, looking for another door, but they all seem to be locked from the outside. I start banging on the walls and shouting for Mr. Willow and finally one of the doors flies open and an old man in a nightshirt wants to know why in the name of thunder I'm making such a ruckus.

"Thanks! Much obliged!" I say, and scoot past him into the passageway, on a dead run for our cabin before it's too late.

But when I get there Mr. Frank Nibbly is already leaning against the wall and studying his fingernails. He gives me a sly little smile and says, "Good evening, Homer. Taking the night air?"

"Where's Mr. Willow?" I demand. "What have you done to him?"

"Mr. Willow is fine," he says. "Mr. Willow is dandy."

Before I can get around him, the cabin door swings open and out steps the Reverend Webster B. Willow in his best frock coat, with Kate Nibbly draped on his arm.

"Mr. Willow, are you okay? Have you still got the money?"

The clergyman has this goofy look on his face, like he's

not sure whether he's in this world or the next, but wherever he is, he's happy to be there. Like he's been hit on the head with a wooden mallet and likes it.

"The most amazing thing has happened," he announces, patting her clever hands. "I am to be married. Miss Nibbly and I are engaged to be married."

18

THE SMELL
OF PIGS

WHAT HAPPENED IS, MISS Nibbly kissed Mr. Willow and he kissed her back, and now he thinks he's obliged to marry her, as a matter of honor.

"I wouldn't expect you to understand such a thing," he says loftily, his eyes shining like little brown pebbles. "What would an orphan boy know of honor?"

Orphan boy. That's what Frank Nibbly called me, and now he's got Mr. Willow saying it, too. Come to think of it, the clergyman hasn't used his own words since he come under the spell of Kate the Beautiful. It's like in the storybooks, where the princess kisses a frog and it turns into a prince, except Mr. Willow has turned into something even dumber than a frog. More like a skinny worm about to be breakfast for a really smart robin.

There's no use talking, because he only hears what he

wants to hear, but that don't stop me speaking my mind on the subject. "You think Mr. Brewster would approve?" I ask him, pacing around the cabin. "He sends you to help me and you get married instead? Have you seen the way her brother looks at your wallet? Like a fox deciding which chicken to eat, that's how he looks!"

"Darling Kate always wanted to be a minister's wife," he says dreamily. "It was love at first sight."

"It was love at first sight, all right! They saw you comin' a mile away. Said to each other, that looks as dumb as a sack of rocks, let's see what he's got in his pockets."

Mr. Willow don't put his fingers in his ears, but he might as well, for all the good it's doing. "We'll settle in New York City, close to her family," he says. "And I shall be pastor of Park Avenue."

"Park Avenue is where the rich folk live, Mr. Willow. Even I heard of that."

"Indeed, indeed. For your information the Nibblys are very wealthy. Dear Frank handles all the finances."

"Dear Frank wants to handle *our* finances, Mr. Willow. You can't let him take the money! We need it to get Harold back."

He ignores me and keeps right on talking his dreamy talk about getting married, the sooner the better.

"I will cable Mr. Brewster from New York and inform him of the happy news," he says, looking off into the distance, as if spotting a lovely rainbow. "He will give me his blessing, I'm sure. Jebediah has been helpful and generous, but the Nibblys are, well, they're the Nibblys."

I never heard of the Nibbly family, but it turns out Mr. Willow knows they're high up in New York society, and it comes to me that it isn't only her beautiful self he loves, but the name attached. It makes me think maybe I'm wrong somehow, because what would a family like that want with a skinny farm boy in a frayed jacket, except if it really is true love?

"We are soul mates," he mutters to himself. "Fate brought us together. Dear Kate has been waiting for me all her life. She knew it the moment she looked into my eyes."

That does it. It can't be true love. Mr. Willow has eyes like a sick kitten. You might love a sick kitten but you don't marry it, you keep it as a pet.

"I've got an idea," I tell him, tugging at his sleeve. "Give me the money. I'll keep it safe until we get to New York."

Mr. Willow looks at me like I crawled out from under a rock. "Trust the money to a poor orphan boy?" he asks, focusing on me like I just came to his attention. "Certainly not. And for that matter, how do we even know you even have a brother? Has anyone seen this so-called brother? Maybe you've been scheming all along to defraud Mr. Brewster. Anything is possible with an orphan boy."

That shuts my mouth. Here I been feeling sorry for poor Mr. Willow, that he's being made a fool of, and all along he's never trusted me. Or maybe it's an idea Frank Nibbly put in his empty head. Doesn't matter how it got there, what scares me is that other folks will believe it, too.

———

MISS NIBBLY PRETENDS TO BE nice about it, but makes it clear that orphan boys are not invited to society weddings.

"Poor boy, you have the attitude of a ruffian," she says, sniffing daintily. "I'm sure it's not your fault, considering your upbringing, but there it is. We can't have ruffians. Ruffians will not be allowed. Ruffians will not be tolerated."

So I'm not just an orphan boy, which is bad enough, I'm a ruffian orphan boy that can't be invited to weddings, or allowed to stay in the cabin when weddings are being planned.

Frank calls in the steward, the one with the funny little hat and the ice-chip eyes, and tells him to remove me from the premises.

"The boy will be happier in steerage," Frank says. "Among his own kind."

The steward grabs hold of my collar.

"I'll tell the captain!" I shout, threatening to expose their evil plan. "I'll tell him how you tricked Mr. Willow, and that you're both liars!"

Kate sighs and rolls her eyes. "What the captain may or may not think is no concern of ours. We have no need of the captain. My brother is a duly licensed justice of the peace. He shall marry us, isn't that right, Frank?"

Frank smiles and consults his pocket watch. "The hour is upon us, Mr. Willow. Are you ready to tie the knot?"

I saw a man in Pine Swamp once who had been kicked in the head by a horse and nearly died. He had a look about him, like he could see all the way to Heaven, and didn't care about this world no more. That's how Mr. Willow looks when he takes Kate's hand.

"You're making a terrible—!"

I mean to say "terrible mistake," but the sneering steward clamps a hand across my mouth and yanks me out of the cabin and shuts the door behind us.

"Do you want to live?" the steward hisses, trotting me along the passageway. "If you want to live, shut your filthy little mouth."

That's when I bite him on the hand, as hard as I can. The steward yelps and drops me and then I'm running full steam for the exit.

"Rotten brat!" he shrieks, reaching out to grab me.

I'd have gotten away for sure, except for the slippery deck. I'm coming around a corner, heading for the door to the deck, when I hit a waxy spot and crash headfirst into an iron pipe.

That's the last thing I remember, the pipe coming at me like a big gray bullet, and then nothing but darkness, and the smell of pigs.

19

THE AMAZING
PIG BOY

FOLKS IN PINE SWAMP LIKE to tell the one about Silas Wiggin, who used to work at the dry-goods store. How Silas loved pork above all things. Ham, ribs, chops, cutlets, bacon, fried cracklings, liver and kidney and pickled trotters—if it wasn't pork Silas wouldn't eat it. The pigs must have loved him, too, and proved it one Saturday night when he came stumbling home the worse for corn liquor, and made the mistake of passing out in the pig sty.

Hogs ate him. Nothing left but his hat and boots.

The story of Silas Wiggin comes to mind when I wake up in the smelly dark with a pig licking at my foot. I kick at the little pig and it scurries to the far side of the crate and commences to squealing. The other pigs join right in.

I'm in a pig crate deep inside the ship, trapped with the livestock.

"Help!" I shout. "Down here! Help! Help!"

With all the noise from the pigs and chickens, it takes me

a while to notice the big steam engine has ceased thumping. Feels like the ship has stopped moving, too.

"Help! Help! Somebody help me!"

I scream and shout for an hour or more, until my throat is so sore and dry I can't get a word out. My head aches from where it crashed into the pipe, and my belly hurts from not eating, and I'm thirsty and exhausted but fearful of falling asleep. Wishing I was back in the barn, sleeping on a pile of nice clean hay. Squinton Leach used to beat us and starve us, but he never fed us to the pigs. Good old Squint, I'd take him over Frank Nibbly any day. Or Mr. Willow for that matter.

After about a hundred years of feeling miserable and scared, there comes a loud rumble as the hatch lifts from the deck. Daylight pours into the hold. This would be a good time to scream and shout for help but my voice is gone, wasted on the dark. All I can do is cling to the slats and make pitiful little noises as the crate is lifted out of the hold and swung up over the side of the ship and set down on the docks with the other crates of livestock.

The pigs are squealing so loud that somebody kicks the side of the crate and yells, "Settle down, you miserable critters!"

I manage to get my hand through the slats and tug on his trouser leg. Next thing a big, red, whiskery face is up close, studying me. "Holy smokin' chimney!" he exclaims, leaping back. "That pig looks just like a boy!"

"Eew, eew," I croak, pointing at my throat, trying to let him know my voice don't work.

"Sam! Jack! Ezra! Come take a look at this!"

Soon enough a crowd gathers to gawk.

"I heard of children raised by wolves," someone says. "This the first I seen raised by pigs."

"Poor creature never learned to speak, so all he can do is croak and squeal."

"Maybe he's really half pig—he's dirty enough."

"Check his feet, see if he's got hooves!"

"Oh look, the little thing is getting mad. Squeal, little pig boy, squeal!"

They start poking sticks into the cage to torment me. I grab one and poke back, which makes them all laugh. I'm spittin' mad, but my throat is still too ragged and sore to get a word out. All I can manage is some noises that probably sound like oinks, which only makes things worse.

"Squeal!" they shout, urging me on. "Squeal!"

Somebody pokes another stick at my face and I snatch it away with my teeth, just like an animal.

"Look at him snarl! The pig boy has strong teeth. Good thing he's in the crate!"

My tormentors are dockworkers and merchantmen and sailors and a few boys not much older than me. One of the boys has been sent to feed the pigs a pail of slops but decides it'd be more fun to throw the stuff at me. Getting spattered with rotten vegetables don't improve my mood. I shriek and spit and bare my teeth. Before long they're backing away, fear in their eyes, half convinced I've got rabies like a mad dog.

Can't talk but I can snarl, and when a hand comes near the crate I snap at it, *grr grr,* just like the animal they think I am.

Now the crowd of onlookers is laughing themselves silly. They've never seen anything as funny as the amazing pig boy. The kid who threw the garbage gets inspired enough to go fetch another pail of slops.

When he slings the bucket at me, everybody applauds and cheers.

"Eat, pig boy! Eat!" they all chant.

I'm wiping garbage off my face when a pair of knee-high polished boots strides up to the side of the crate. Can't quite see the owner of that fine pair of boots, but he makes himself heard soon enough.

"Who's in charge here?" the boot man demands. "Who does this boy belong to? Speak up! You're mighty free with your taunts but you can't answer a simple question, is that it? I ask again, who is in charge of this boy?"

The big man with the whiskery red face scowls and folds his arms. "Who wants to know?"

"Fenton J. Fleabottom, Professor," he announces, and as he scrapes and bows, sweeping away a stovepipe top hat, I catch a glimpse of a long narrow face, a curly blond mustache, and lively gray eyes that sparkle with mischief. "And who are you, my good sir? Is this your crate? Are these your pigs?"

The man won't give his name. "The pigs are mine, right enough."

"And the boy?"

"Never seen him before."

"Never seen him? Remarkable. Raised him with your pigs, but never noticed he was a boy?"

"Yur twistin' my words!"

Professor Fleabottom squares up with his hands on his hips. "Consider yourself fortunate that I don't twist your pimpled nose," he says in a voice so powerful and command-ing that the crowd of tormentors starts to melt away, as if shameful of what they've done. "If I hadn't just had these boots polished I would kick your pig-smelling backside from here to New Jersey. Now unlock this crate before I whistle for the coppers and have you arrested!"

The man hurries over, and a moment later the side of the crate falls away. The little pigs stay huddled in the corner, but I scoot out and crawl to my feet, stinking of garbage and manure. I never felt so miserable and empty and mad all at once, and when the red-faced man sees the anger in my eyes he backs slowly away.

"Bring a bucket of clean water!" Professor Fleabottom demands.

It takes more than one bucket to rinse off the smell of pigs. They soak me down until I'm drenched. Then Professor

Fleabottom hands me a ladle of cool, clean water, and the soothing drink eases my throat and brings my voice back. I'm able to look up at Professor Fleabottom and say, "Thank you, sir," like a real human being.

Fenton J. Fleabottom doffs his tall stovepipe hat and makes a short bow from the waist. "I am yours to command, young man," he says. "Remarkable act you've got! You play an outraged swine like you were born to the part. A rare talent indeed. Tell me, young man, are you otherwise engaged?"

Turns out Professor Fleabottom owns a traveling medicine show, and he wants to hire me.

"Our geek just died, poor fellow. Choked on a chicken head," he says. Seeing the look on my face, he adds, "Don't worry, my boy, you needn't bite the heads off live chickens. Any small bird will do."

20

THE CARAVAN
OF MIRACLES

PROFESSOR FLEABOTTOM has a way of listening that makes you think he really and truly wants to hear what you have to say. It's something about the way his kindly, humorous eyes seem to soak up every word, eager for more. Even his waxed yellow mustache looks interested, the way it quivers as he listens. Before I know it I've told him all about Uncle Squint, and how he made me and Harold live in the barn and work ourselves to the bone and never fed us proper, and how Squint sold Harold to the army, and how I aim to save him from dying in the war, because Harold is so true and brave he's bound to be killed. I tell him about the clergyman Webster B. Willow and the horrible Nibblys, and how they stole a sum of money intended to buy my brother out of the army and had me put in with the pigs.

When I'm done talking, and feeling more than a little sorry for myself, Fleabottom pats me on the head and says,

"That's quite a story. I especially liked the part where you single-handedly defeated fifty bounty hunters and freed a thousand slaves."

"There was others that helped," I grudgingly admit. "Jebediah Brewster and Samuel Reed pitched in."

"Sometimes the truth works best when simplified," Professor Fleabottom allows, with a twinkle in his eyes. "Now then, having heard your amazing tale, I wish to make three observations. First, if you are still determined to find your brother, then we may be of use to each other, for I go where the army goes."

"To fight in the war?" I ask, staring at his curled-up mustache.

He chuckles and shakes his head. "We go to turn a dollar," he says. "The money is where the army is."

"I've got money, if only we can find Mr. Willow."

Fleabottom shakes his head, looking very serious. "Listen to one who knows, Homer," he says. "That money is long gone. The pair you describe are professional thieves. There are many like them, working the ferry terminals and train stations, preying upon innocent men like your Mr. Willow. It is an old ruse. The marriage was undoubtedly phony, an excuse to pick his pocket. By now they will have taken the money and dispensed with him. Truly, I'm surprised he didn't end up in the same crate as you."

"Can you really help me find my brother?"

Fleabottom shrugs. "I can only promise to try. Because of

the nature of my business, I have certain associates in uniform. I give you my word of honor. I will ask after Harold Figg, newly recruited, and we shall see what comes of it."

I got my doubts about words of honor. Mr. Willow swore on a Bible, and pledged his word to Jebediah Brewster, and look where it got me. But I fear what Professor Fleabottom says is true. The money is gone. If I want to save Harold from the army I've got to find him on my own, or with whatever help I can manage.

"My second observation," says Professor Fleabottom, "is that your experience living in a barn may be useful. The close proximity of a few small swine should be tolerable."

"I don't mind a pig," I admit. "Unless it tries to eat me."

"Ah! We will endeavor with all our powers to make sure that does not happen," he promises grandly. "My third and final observation is that you need a proper bath. The pungent perfume of the pig is still upon you. The suffocating scent of the swine exudes from your person. In a word, sir, you stink."

Professor Fleabottom guides me along the crowded waterfront, past gangs of men swarming over ships and barges, to where his wagons have been unloaded from a Boston steamship. Each of the three brightly painted wagons has a team of two horses, and the nags look none too frisky. I'd been hoping to see an elephant or at the very least a proper lion, but he explains that his is not a large animal show.

"We are small in everything but spirit," he adds brightly.

"The Fleabottom Caravan of Miracles is but a humble attempt to entertain our brave troops, providing temporary release from the horrors of war, and such medicines as are needed. In this we do our duty, as citizens of the republic."

"What kind of medicine do you sell?" I ask.

"The best kind of medicine," he says. "The kind that makes you smile."

I never been to a real traveling medicine show because Squint naturally hates such things, but Harold saw one when our Dear Mother still lived, and said they had a mermaid girl with fish scales on her skin, and a two-headed snake in a jar, and a man that played the banjo with his feet. After the show they sold bottles of Neurotonic Nerve Elixir that was as powerful as sweetened rum, and smelled pretty much the same. Harold said it was a splendid good time even if Mother refused to let him sample the medicine.

"Minerva!" Professor Fleabottom shouts. "Show yourself, my dear!"

A wagon door opens and out comes a skinny woman with hair so red it looks like her head's on fire. The fiery hair's not the best thing about her though. She's wearing a sleeveless, tight-waisted gown and every inch of her arms is covered with colorful ink drawings, right down to the fingertips. I never seen a genuine tattooed lady before, and it is truly an impressive sight. The drawings move up her arms like pictures in a book and make me want to know the story they tell.

"As a child of twelve, shipwrecked upon a cannibal island,

Mini was taken as captive in the South Seas," Fleabottom explains. "The savages marked her as one of their own."

The red-haired lady rolls her eyes and says, "Save it for the pitch, Fenton." Then she wrinkles her skinny nose and makes a face. "Whew! What did you step in? Best check your boots."

"Pigs, my dear," he says cheerfully. "Would you be so good as to see this young man gets a hot bath and fresh clothing?"

She gives me a cautious look. "Does he bite?"

"Only when provoked. Avoid poking him with sticks and you'll be quite safe."

"Hot water is ten cents a tub," she says, sounding outraged about the price. "And five cents for soap!"

Professor Fleabottom reaches into his waistcoat pocket and hands her some coins. "Well worth the investment, as you shall see. The boy has talent, Minerva, real talent. His lies are as sweet as honey and twice as smooth. Clean him up and let's get this show on the road!"

21

BOILED
BY INDIANS

FAR AS I'M CONCERNED, taking a bath is sort of like drowning, with soap. Never could abide it, not since I was a little baby. Harold says our Dear Mother used to rinse me in a big tin pot under the water pump, like I was a potato, and it always made me holler. So naturally I try to persuade Minerva, the tattooed lady, to save the ten cents and buy us some taffy and licorice twists instead, and maybe a peppermint to improve her breath.

"Bath is a waste of time, money, and effort," I'm saying as she drags me into an alley not far from the steamship terminal. The alley is a dim and narrow place of falling-down shacks and skinny buildings that lean toward the harbor. "A little dirt makes a person healthy," I insist. "Look, all I got to do is spit on my hands and rub 'em on my trousers. See? Good as new."

She gives me a look that would make a weasel die of shame. "One, it's Professor Fleabottom's money and we shan't be spending it on candy. Two, hold your tongue or that will get a taste of soap, too. Understood?"

"What about three?"

"Three?"

"When a person says one something, and two this or that, usually they say three such and such. It's never just one and two, there's always a three."

Everybody knows that red-haired folks tend to excite easily, and that's certainly the case with the tattooed lady. Without another word — sputtering don't count — she slings me over her hip like a sack of laundry and before I can count to four we're inside a hot, steamy shack and she's handed me over to the Indians for boiling.

The Indians plunge me into a big wooden laundry tub of hot soapy water and scrub me like a load of dirty shirts, and talk to each other in a language that sounds like a bag of bells falling down the stairs. Turns out they're not Indians like we have in Maine, that mostly live in the woods and fish and hunt. These are Indians from China — similar eyes, but a different tribe.

"Best behave yourself," Minerva warns, as they dry me off with fluffy towels, and dress me in clean clothes. "If I tell them you're half pig, they might have you for supper."

Apparently being shipwrecked on a cannibal island makes Minerva think all foreigners are cannibals.

"For your information, Indians don't eat children," I tell her. "They prefer full-growed females with red hair."

I figure that will embarrass the tattooed lady, or at least make steam come out of her ears. But much to my surprise, instead of getting mad, she laughs.

"Fenton's right," she says, chuckling. "You are a funny one." On the way back she buys me a bag of taffy candy, and a peppermint for herself. "To improve my breath," she says, still laughing.

———

BACK AT THE STEAMSHIP terminal Professor Fleabottom has the wagons ready to go and seems mighty eager to be shut of this particular area.

"There are skulkers about," he tells Minerva, his mustache all twitchy with nerves.

"You mean coppers," she says brightly. "Where are they?"

"Not coppers," he says, keeping his voice low. "Spies. All around. Here and there. They're very clever spies."

"Spies?" she says loudly. "And why ever would spies be interested in us?"

Fleabottom puts a finger to his lips. "Hush, woman. The world has ears."

Then he notices me standing there, listening to every word.

"Bad habit of mine," he says, clearing his throat. "Joking about this and that. What a ridiculous idea!"

He goes on for a while, laughing and pretending the stuff about skulkers and spies is just a prank, but I know a thing or two about stretching the truth, and Mr. Fenton J. Fleabottom, he's a stretcher.

I decide to keep my eyes peeled, just in case.

22

THE SECRET
IN THE WAGONS

PROFESSOR FLEABOTTOM lets me ride next to him, high up in the driver's seat as the horses plod through the crowded streets, headed for the ferry terminal.

Never have I seen so many people in one place, all trying to get somewhere at the same time. Folks of all colors, white and black and mixed, and a bunch that look like the Chinese Indians, and others I never seen before. Men in fine suits and tall hats, and ladies with parasols and gloves, and men in rags, and poor, hunched-up old women begging as they shuffle along. All in a hurry. Makes me feel a little out of breath to think that if one more human being sets foot on this end of Manhattan Island, it may tip over like a dinner plate and slip into the sea.

Professor Fleabottom says there's more people in this city than in the entire state of Maine, all jammed together with a hundred thousand horses, and more goats, dogs, cats, cows, and chickens than can be counted. All breathing the same smoky air and drinking the same water.

The horses, he says, are a special kind of problem.

"Multiply a hundred thousand horses by twenty pounds of manure each day, per horse, and what do you get?"

"A big stink?"

"On the nose!" he says, delighted. "Two thousand tons of odiferous delight. All of which makes me long for the fragrance of New Jersey."

"What's New Jersey smell like?"

"Grass and dirt, mostly, once we get past the swampy part. But first we must cross the river."

Every now and then he looks behind, as if worried about being followed. I check, too, but there are so many people there's no way to know who might be following us, or who might just be going in the same direction.

Wagons scrape by, heading the opposite way, and the big men driving the wagons crack their whips and shout abuse and make rude gestures.

Professor Fleabottom smiles and waves, and tells Minerva to stay out of sight inside the wagon, in case her tattoos might stop traffic altogether.

"Just drive, Fenton. I can take care of myself, as well you know," she says, looking around.

Seems like even though she made fun of him for mentioning spies, she's keeping an eye out, too.

As for me, I'm straining to catch a glimpse of the men

driving the last two wagons in our little caravan. From what I can see, as we jounce over the cobblestones, they both look pretty normal. Just regular men with beards and floppy hats that hide their eyes.

"Sit down and quit messing about," Professor Fleabottom says. "You'll scare the horses."

"What's in those wagons?" I want to know.

The way Fleabottom and Minerva are acting, there might be something hidden in the wagons. Something way more exciting than a boy who pretends to be a pig.

"Ah!" Fleabottom says, his eyes glinting with humor. "You guessed, did you?"

"I guessed there was something, but I don't know what, exactly."

"Patience, young man. You will know all of our secrets by this evening. But not until then."

No matter how much I beg, he won't tell me the secret in the wagons, and finally I decide to shut up and bide my chance.

The ferry terminal is near as crowded as the streets, with a mob waiting impatiently to get across the Hudson River. Some are on foot, others in carriages and wagons. The ferries leave on the quarter hour, regular as clockwork. They have flat decks so you can drive straight aboard, and big steam-driven paddles on either side.

At the sounding of a steam whistle the gate opens and a man shouts, "All aboard!"

Ten minutes later, wagons and horses and all, we're bound for Jersey City.

The river is thick with ferryboats and steamships and sailboats of every size. Looks like the whole world is on the move, crossing that water. Behind us the island of Manhattan starts to fade away, until it looks like it's made of fog and sticks. The puffs of gray smoke tooting out of the ferryboat smokestack reminds me of Uncle Squint's clay pipe. Makes me wonder if he misses us. Most likely he misses all the work we did.

Strange as it may seem, I sort of miss the farm. The barn that was our home, and Bob the horse, and Bess and Floss the milk cows. Can't say as I miss Squint himself in particular. No surprise there. The real surprise is waiting on the dock in New Jersey, standing tall in his new blue uniform.

My brother, Harold, big as life.

23

THE SOUND
OF GUNS

SOON AS THE FERRY BUMPS the pier I'm off and running, thinking this surely is my lucky day. My adventures
have barely begun and already I've found my big brother! It
wasn't so bad, just an abduction or two, and being robbed
and thrown in with the pigs, and joining the Caravan of
Miracles, and being boiled by Indians.

Already I'm improving the story in my mind, with the
purpose of making Harold laugh. He don't laugh that much,
being a serious-minded person, but when he does, it feels
like someone gave you a silver dollar, because it's bright and
shiny and rings true. I come all this way just to hear it.

"Harold! Harold! It's me, Homer!"

I fight my way through a sea of young men in new uniforms. Dark blue, four-button coats and sky blue trousers
and forage caps, and each man with a black canvas haver-

sack to carry his food. Most of the Union Army seems to be milling about, waiting for trains to take them south. It's like a blue wool forest that smells of sweat and boot polish.

Figure if I can get to Harold before he gets on a war train we can fix it so he don't have to go. We being me and Professor Fleabottom, since he knows men in the army and can maybe help us.

"Harold! Harold!"

At last he turns to my voice.

Up close, the face is wrong. My stomach flip-flops something awful and I nearly trip and fall, because it ain't Harold. It's another boy who could be him, on account of his size and the way he stands.

"You're . . . not . . . Harold!" I say, stopping to catch my breath.

"Private Thomas Finch, Fifteenth Massachusetts," he says, voice cracking.

"Sorry. Looking for my brother. Harold Figg. Of Pine Swamp, Maine."

Private Finch shakes his head. "I believe the Maine regiments that mustered here have gone ahead. Your brother may be among them."

"Okay," I pant, blinking the sweat from my eyes. "Thanks."

I'm about to go find Professor Fleabottom and the wagons, when I'm struck by inspiration. "Private Finch," I say, turning back to tug at his stiff woolen sleeve. "If you happen to come across Harold Figg of Pine Swamp, Maine, would you please tell him to get on home? His little brother, Homer, is dying. Will you tell him that?"

"If I meet him, certainly," says Private Finch. "But it is a big war. How will I know him?"

"Looks a lot like you, except Harold is slightly taller and stronger and better looking."

"Is that a fact?" says Private Finch with a toothy grin. "I'll see what I can do, Homer. You are Homer Figg, right?"

I shrug. "Maybe I am."

"I must say, my young friend, that you look remarkably healthy for a boy who is dying."

"Never mind that. Will you tell him?"

"Of course."

After glancing around and grinning to himself, he snaps me a fine salute. "Thank you, Homer Figg. I am reminded to write a letter to my own dear little brother, who is slightly taller and stronger and better looking than you, and who would no doubt fake his own death to have me safe at home."

He melts away into the blue wool forest.

A moment later the tattooed lady has me by the collar. She's puffing like I am, from fighting her way through the crowd.

"Thought we'd lost you, boy!" She tips up my chin, looks me in the eye. "What's this, have you been crying?"

I shake my head and she knows enough to say no more.

THAT EVENING THE CARAVAN of Miracles puts on the first show since I joined the company. We're ten hard miles from the terminal in Jersey City, in low, weedy country not far from the sea, and come upon an army encampment. Must be a hundred white canvas tents set up in the tall grass, and the sound of rolling gunfire and shouting men just over the horizon.

"Is there a battle?" I want to know, standing up in my seat to see better. "Is this the war?"

"The war is still some great distance away," Professor Fleabottom explains. "These are new recruits, training to fight."

We set up our wagons in a little area surrounded by sandy bluffs, which he says is to keep us from the wind, but which also means we're hard to see if you don't know where to look.

"A medicine show is not always welcomed by the generals," he tells me. "They think it distracts from the business of war. Whereas we believe that these young men deserve a bit of fun at the end of a long, hard day. Thus we strive to entertain, but with the utmost discretion."

While we unload gear and get ready for the show, the two men who drive the other wagons approach the army camp on foot, and let the recruits know where we are, and what might be expected of us.

Me and Minerva are in charge of setting out the lamps

and torches for when it gets dark and putting up the banners and flags.

A warm wind lifts the silky banners and makes it look like the words are dancing on air.

Fleabottom's Miracle Elixir!

The Totally Tattooed Lady from Cannibal Island!

The Talented Tumbling Brillo Brothers!

The Amazing Pig Boy!

The really amazing thing is, I can't wait to see the show, and I'm in it.

24

THREE OINKS
FOR HOMER PIG

WHEN THE LAST BLUE TWILIGHT finally fades from the evening sky, soldiers begin to arrive in groups of two or three, whispering to one another and laughing quietly. They're not supposed to be here, watching a medicine show, but are meant to be back in their tents fast asleep.

"One evening is all we spend at any encampment," Mini explains, covering up her tattooed arms with long, puffy, clip-on sleeves. "Folks like us, traveling kinds of people, we must keep moving or the law will catch us."

"What we're doing, selling bottles of medicine, that's against the law?"

"Not exactly," she says uneasily, not meeting my eyes. "It's more that strangers are never truly welcome, not for long."

When the show begins, we're inside the main wagon — Mini, because she's putting on her long sleeves, and me, because I'm the Amazing Pig Boy and can't show my face until the end.

Peeking out through the canvas, I watch as Professor Fleabottom claps his hands and leaps up on a little wooden platform that tips down from the side of the wagon.

His hat is tall, his knee-high boots are polished like black glass, and the buttons on his coat are five-dollar gold pieces that glow like little suns in the light of the oil lanterns.

"Good evening to all you brave gentlemen! Welcome to the Caravan of Miracles! May Almighty God bless the Union Army and deliver it from losing, time and again! With all you new recruits being trained to kill your fellow man, surely victory will soon follow! And to help you along the way, to ease the woes and pains of the battlefield, and the pinch of bedbugs in your soggy tents, and to improve the taste of the insects that infest your food, and, frankly, to give you courage when most needed, I, Professor Fenton J. Fleabottom, honored graduate of ancient universities in the Far East, have perfected a certain strong elixir. An elixir that will lift your spirits and put the gleam back in your eyes! An elixir containing a sure cure for what ails you! An elixir that will, from the very first sip, deliver you from evil, and place you in the soft, motherly bosom of mankind!"

A murmur comes from the crowd of young soldiers, and many raise up their hands, as if to grasp at invisible bottles.

"Patience, young heroes! Patience! Patience! The elixir goes on sale following the show, and not a moment before. Have no fear, there's plenty for everyone! Now, if one of you good fellows will hand up that banjo, I will demonstrate how a single dose of Fleabottom's Miracle Elixir cured my rheumatic joints, improved the dexterity of my digits, and clarified my ears. Listen and be amazed!"

The professor then commences to flail upon the banjo. It starts out as a sad and mournful tune, a slow version of "Rally 'Round the Flag, Boys," but then he starts speeding things up and really making that old banjo ring. The soldiers begin to clap along, some of them singing, and just when you think the song is done, Mini slips behind him and somehow takes the banjo from him and keeps strumming without missing a beat.

How the men cheer! Mini gives them a wild grin and plays a lot of high plinky notes that sound like metal sparks exploding from fireworks, and then somehow she and the professor are *both* bashing at the banjo, Mini with her fingers on the frets and Fleabottom plucking the strings with hands that move so fast his fingers are blurred.

I never heard anything near so exciting as four-handed banjo, and it's all I can do to stay in the wagon instead of leaping out and joining the crowd. When the song finally comes to an end, Mini and the professor hold hands and take a bow, and the soldiers erupt in applause.

In Pine Swamp, that trick with the banjo would be good

for a year's worth of entertainment, but the Caravan of Miracles is just getting warmed up. Before the cheering stops, two wild men leap out of nowhere, juggling flaming torches and whistling between their teeth.

The Talented Tumbling Brillo Brothers are the bearded guys who drive the other two wagons. Mini told me their true name isn't Brillo, which is something the professor made up, but they really are brothers and can tumble about like chipmunks and juggle anything that comes to hand — flaming torches, then some wooden buckets, then bricks, then boxes and bricks, and even three small chairs.

At the end they grab a small soldier from the crowd — a drummer boy not much bigger than me — and they juggle *him*, much to the amusement of his friends.

After the Talented Tumbling Brillo Brothers take their bows, Professor Fleabottom resumes his place upon the stage.

"Gentlemen! As the great Roman warrior Marc Antony once famously said, 'Lend me your ears!' For I have a tale to tell. A curious tale of woe. A tantalizing tale of tragedy. A strange tale that begins in the great north woods of Maine, where the bear and the moose frolic in pine forests whose feathery tops reach near enough to Heaven. In forests dark and dense, where the wolves are as black as moon shadows, and white men's feet have yet to trod the ancient earth. In just such a place a rare and unusual creature was recently discovered by a band of kindly Indians. The Indians found, cowering and snarling in one of their traps, a creature the ancients called a chimera. A hybrid creature, part human, part hog. Half boy, half pig. Do you not believe? Do I sense emanations of doubt? Are there skeptics among you? Then, gentlemen, prepare to be amazed. I give you . . . the Amazing Pig Boy!"

His mighty voice ringing in the night, the professor lifts high his lantern as the crate is trundled out of the wagon.

In the crate are three squealing, frightened little pigs. Three pigs and me, and I'm squealing, too, and snuffling my dirty nose around the slats of the crate and baring my teeth and pretending I'll bite any hand that strays too near.

"Stand back, gentlemen! Back, I say! Be warned, the creature bites! Last week it chomped a hand clean off at the wrist! It has bitten off noses, ears, and once took the last eyeball from a one-eyed sailor!"

I'm naked except for a pair of skimpy drawers, but it don't hardly matter because I'm so caked with filth that none of my skin shows through—it's like wearing a dirt suit. Mini helped me stuff leaves in my hair to puff out my ears, and glued a little curly tail on my backside. When she held up a little mirror, to admire our work, I nearly screamed.

The savage beast in the mirror wasn't me. It couldn't be, could it?

Fact is, I'm scaring myself half to death. Not just because I'm so filthy and ferocious looking, but because it's fun being a pig boy.

I like wiggling my glued-on tail.

I like baring my teeth and squealing like a trapped animal.

I like scaring soldiers who are twice as old as me, and who leap back like frightened children when I snap at their fingers.

It's fun to be amazing, to be the star of the show, to have everyone watching you — even if you have to act like a pig. And before long, I really do feel more animal than human.

"Watch out there, he'll take your hand off!" cries a young soldier, backing away.

My brain is screaming to be let out of the crate, so I can bite all my tormentors. But instead of screaming words, I'm screaming pig noises.

"Rage, you poor creature!" the professor bellows, gesturing with the lantern. "Rage at the tragedy of your existence! Rage and squeal against the indignity of your fetid prison!"

He turns to the astonished crowd, putting a hand upon his heart. "Gentlemen, I ask you this: A half-breed creature, a thing neither one nor the other, is a thing such as this, endowed with a soul? When it dies, will it meet its Maker, or shall it return to the dust? A man has a soul and an animal does not, this we have been taught. But what of a half man? Has it half a soul, or none at all?"

The soldiers get real quiet. Only thing making noise is me. *Oink, oink, oink.*

"Only God knows the answer," the professor announces, very grand and solemn. "Take this poor creature away!" he says, calling for the Brillo Brothers. "Hide it from human eyes! Gentlemen, there is no cure for the Amazing Pig Boy, but be assured there is ample cure for each and every one of you!"

The Brillo Brothers throw a rug over my crate and sling it back into the wagon.

As Mini hands out the bottles, the professor's golden voice booms into the night.

"Gather round! Fleabottom's Miracle Elixir will cure what ails you! Satisfaction guaranteed! One dollar the bottle, boys! A dollar well spent! And for each that buys a bottle, a glimpse of the Totally Tattooed Lady from Cannibal Island!"

Back inside the wagon, a bucket of soapy water awaits, so that I may clean up and become human again. Lifting the canvas, I glimpse the soldiers upending the elixir bottles, their eyes glazed in the lantern light.

Even covered with pig filth, I can smell the "medicine" we're selling.

I know that smell.

Whiskey.

Professor Fleabottom's Miracle Elixir is just plain whiskey.

25

SEE THE ELEPHANT
AND DIE

WHEN I WAS NINE YEARS OLD, Harold snuck me to the state fair in Skowhegan. I say *snuck* because old Squint forbade us going, on account of the evil influences common at fairs. Meaning, I guess, that folks have fun, and that can't be good, not so far as Squint was concerned. In his opinion humans were best when miserable, and so he had worked at being miserable his whole life, and in his generous way tried to make as many people miserable as possible.

The Skowhegan fairgrounds being some distance away, Harold persuaded one of the Pine Swamp farmers to carry us there in the back of his vegetable cart. Wouldn't you know the cart threw a wheel and we ended up walking most of twenty miles. I kept wanting to turn back, on account of my feet hurting, but Harold wouldn't let me give up.

When we got there, it was worth it. I'd never seen so

many people in one place. Most every tent and booth had food to sell. Fried dough with sugar frosting, and hot doughnuts with cinnamon sprinkles, and roasted beef and chicken wings, and pickled eels and herring, and sugared this and honeyed that, and even though we didn't have money, we ate our fill of what others left behind.

Ate so much I got sick, but I didn't care—I kept right on eating!

There was harness racing around a big dirt track, with folks screaming and waving tickets, and exhibitions of fine carriages and farm equipment, and draft horses hauling tons of stone from the quarry, and prize livestock, and late at night a special tent where women danced in their underclothes and showed their bare ankles.

That's where I first smelled whiskey breathing from a crowd, outside the dancing-girls tent. We was forbidden to enter, of course, being only boys, but stationed ourselves outside because some of the men were so drunk they needed help to walk and paid us a penny to assist them to their wagons, so's they wouldn't have to sleep in the mud.

That's where I learned that whiskey makes men stupid, there at the Skowhegan Fair.

Makes men stupid in New Jersey, too. Draining their bottles of "medicine" like it was water and they was dying of thirst. Some stand swaying, others fall to their knees. Some laugh at nothing, others weep for their mothers, sick for home.

It don't seem right to me, getting soldiers drunk, but Professor Fleabottom says I must get used to it if I have any hope of finding Harold.

"These boys, every last one of them, they're all replacements. Do you know what a replacement is?" he asks me. When I shake my head he says, "It means that in a few weeks they will take the place of those who have died in battle, or from disease, and many of them will perish, too. The elixir gives them courage, if only for a little while."

"Some are puking, sir."

He shrugs. "They'll puke on the battlefield, too. War is an awful thing, Homer. Whiskey is just whiskey. We serve a purpose whether you know it or not."

"Yes, sir."

"Tonight they saw the Amazing Pig Boy and got a little drunk. Before the summer is over they'll have seen the elephant, and many will have seen the grave."

"Yes, sir."

"Seeing the elephant" is soldier-talk for fighting in a battle.

I'm praying Harold never sees the elephant.

WE HIT THE ROAD HARD for two long weeks. Each day putting miles of dust behind us, and every night setting up not far from some army encampment or other, and then packing up and fleeing when the show is over. Sometimes I ride with the professor or Mini, other times with the jugglers. The jugglers — Bernard and Tallyrand, that's their real names — at first seem full of jokes and pranking. But after a while I come to understand they're worried they'll be swept up by the draft if they stay in one place too long.

"Nothing to fear, brother," says Bern, as we plod along the road, heading south. "The army gets us, we'll juggle cannon balls. Or catch bullets in our teeth."

"More likely in our brains," says Tally, rolling his eyes.

"We have brains?" says Bern.

"Small ones," says Tally. "Not smart enough to think, just dumb enough to juggle."

Tally don't only juggle, he's also the caravan cook, and a mighty good one, too. He can cook potatoes six different ways, and fry up chicken in a deep iron skillet, and he makes a thing called womper that's like beef stew inside a crust. My favorite, though, is eggs, sausage, and biscuits. That one's good not only for breakfast, but any time of day or night.

One time the brothers have a hankering for a late-night snack of pork chops, and Tally asks would I mind giving up one of the little pigs that share my crate.

"Over my dead body!" I tell him, my ears getting hot. "Would you fry up Bernard, just because you were hungry? You leave my friends alone!"

Bern chuckles and shakes his head. "Told you he's thinkin' like a pig. That's why he's so convincing."

"That and the tail," says Tally.

PROFESSOR FLEABOTTOM proves to be as good as his word, asking after Harold at every army camp we visit and trying to determine where he might be posted. Most of the soldiers we meet are from New Jersey or New York, but twice we come upon troops intended for Maine regiments.

Much to my disappointment my brother is not among them.

A grizzled-looking, Portland-born sergeant tells us that many of the new recruits are promised to the 20th Maine, to replace those felled by an outbreak of smallpox. He spits about a quart of tobacco juice in one squirt, wipes his beard with his sleeve. "After beating the Union at Chancellorsville, Lee has left Virginia and headed north," he says. "That's what we hear. Nobody tells us nothin', a-course, so it's mostly rumor and lies."

"Indeed?" the professor says, sounding very interested. "General Lee comes north?"

Robert E. Lee is the wily old Confederate general that's been winning most of the battles ever since the war started, and even the toughest Union men speak of him with respect.

The sergeant squints at the professor. "Could be," he says. "What makes you so curious? Wouldn't happen to be spying, would you?"

The professor laughs and slaps his knee. "Good one, sir! I may be hanged for a rascal, but never a spy! No, no, sir, our curiosity is perfectly innocent! We ask because this orphan boy is looking for his brother. Claims he was illegally sold into the army at the tender age of seventeen."

"Was he now?" The sergeant studies me with his squinty eyes.

"Yes, sir, my uncle said he was twenty and swore him in for replacement and kept the money. That swear was a dirty lie. Harold ain't but seventeen."

"And what do you aim to do, little fella, supposin' you do find him? He's been swore in, you said so yourself."

"I don't know," I admit. "But find him I must."

The sergeant gives another suspicious glance to the professor, then jerks his chin at me. "Try Pennsylvania, vicinity of the Potomac River. Any men mustered in the last few months, that's likely where they'll send 'em, in preparation for the battle to come. And, son?"

"Yes, sir?"

"Keep your head down. Soon enough the air will be thick with lead."

That night I can't sleep for worrying about Harold. He's so strong and brave they've probably given him the flag to carry into battle. First thing those Confederates will see is Harold coming over the hill, waving the Stars and Stripes, and every secessionist rifle will have eyes for him.

I imagine General Robert E. Lee on his gray horse, shooting at Harold with his fancy silver pistol, and Harold falling, tangled up in the flag.

I imagine Harold bleeding on the ground, his face getting paler and paler.

Harold dead.

That's when I get up from my little bunk in the last wagon and climb out into the night, wanting some cool air to clear my head. It's stupid to torment myself with visions of what might happen to my brother when he gets to the war.

Nothing to be done but to keep on searching as our little caravan heads west, into Pennsylvania, like the old sergeant said. Find the Maine regiments and explain to the generals that they got the wrong boy, that they must give me back my big brother before something bad happens.

I'm a few yards from the wagons, doing my business behind a big rock, when the rider comes out of the night.

Man on a black horse. He's got the horse's hooves wrapped in rags, to muffle the sound, and at first I think he must be here to rob us. Why else sneak up on us through the darkest, quietest part of the night?

I'm about ready to shout out a warning to the others when Professor Fleabottom slips out of the first wagon. He's wearing a dark cloak that blends him into the darkness, and something about the way he moves says he's all business.

The professor meets up with the man on the horse. They speak for a few minutes, but so low I can't hear nothing but a murmur. Then Professor Fleabottom looks around to make sure nobody is watching—he don't see me peeking around the rock—and he reaches into the dark cloak and takes out a leather satchel, the kind that carries mail or dispatches.

The professor hands the satchel to the man on the black horse. The man gives him a quick salute and wheels the horse away, vanishing silently into the night.

Now I got two reasons not to sleep: Harold and whatever the professor is up to, sneaking around under cover of darkness.

26

THE TERRIBLE BLACK WAGONS

ABOUT THE ONLY THING I recall about our Dear Mother dying is the coffin. How it smelled of pine and camphor, and how small it was. How was our Dear Mother to sleep in a place so narrow? That worried me so much I could not sleep or eat until Harold explained that our Dear Mother was herself now in Heaven, and had left behind a pale remnant that must be buried in the earth.

The pine box would suffice.

Still I didn't understand. What did he mean by "remnant?"

"A thing left behind," he told me.

"How do you know?" I asked him.

He said, "Mother told me herself, just before she passed. She said we must not grieve over her poor body because it is only a remnant, and her immortal soul has flown off to be with God. She'll have all the room she needs in Heaven, Homer, so you are not to worry."

I was four years old at the time, which means Harold was only nine, but he comforted me better than any grown-up, and I was able to sleep so long as it was next to him, knowing he would be there always.

What makes me think of that little pine box, and Harold, too? The terrible black wagons we meet upon the road, not far from Bethlehem, Pennsylvania. They are like big hay-rick wagons without the hay, drawn by four horses, and the whole of each wagon is swaddled in black cloth and marked with the Union emblem.

Under the cloth, peeking out here and there, are stacks of cheap pine coffins.

The professor pulls our little caravan over to let the death wagons pass, and bides us stand with hats off and heads bowed, as a sign of respect.

As the last wagon goes by, it throws a spoke and nearly overturns. The professor leaps down to offer his assistance and puts Tally and Bern to work repairing the wheel while he entertains the driver with his fine talk.

"A splendid job you're doing, bringing comfort to the bereaved," he says. "How is it these men were not buried on the battlefield?"

"Most are, of course," the driver says, wiping his sweaty brow with a soiled hankie. "These poor brave soldiers died of their wounds sometime after the battle, and so are returned to their homes."

"What battle was this?" the professor wants to know. "We hear only dribs and drabs of the war."

"Skirmishes mostly," the driver says. "The armies are maneuvering, trying to get position."

"Near the Potomac, I suppose?"

The driver shakes his head wearily. "West of the river. Lee has been harassing Harrisburg of late. The Union sends its men to find him and this is how they return—shot to pieces and dying. Some from their wounds, more from sickness and fever. It is a sad business."

"Very sad," says the professor. "Tell me, sir, would a mild tonic help? A pick-me-up?"

He means his elixir and the driver readily accepts. As he sips from the bottle the weary driver becomes even more talkative, and he and the professor discuss the state of the war.

It seems that after their triumph at Chancellorsville the Confederate forces have indeed come north as rumored, invading Pennsylvania and looking to put a bayonet through the heart of the Union Army.

"They say if Lee wins one more battle the war will be over and the South will be triumphant."

"Surely not!" The professor says, looking much distressed. "Our General Hooker can fight, can he not?"

"Hooker?" The driver gives him an odd look as he takes another swig of elixir. "Have you not heard? Fighting Joe Hooker has resigned in despair or bad temper, no one knows for sure. Lincoln has promoted General Meade in his place and ordered him to stop Lee's army at all cost."

"Meade is in charge? Extraordinary!"

"You know something of the Union generals, do you?" the driver asks suspiciously.

The professor clears his throat. "Only what I read in the newspapers. I know nothing of Meade but his name, really."

The driver shrugs. "Ah well. It is not for us to criticize. It is only for us to serve and die as the generals command. They say that some of the northern states are near rebellion themselves. New York in particular. They want an end to things, one way or another. These are the dark days of the war, a time for dying by the thousand, and for what? To free the slaves? I care nothing for slaves!"

After that the driver will speak no more. He waits until his wagon is repaired, then trundles off, silent as the grave.

The professor stands in the road, watching as the coffin wagon rounds a bend and vanishes from sight, then pats me on the head. "Not to worry, young Mr. Figg. If what the man says is true, the war may be over before your brother has to fight."

I hope so. I don't want Harold coming home in no black wagon.

27

THE MAD
BALLOON MAN

ONE FINE DAY, NOT FAR from Lancaster, Pennsylvania, the wind brings us a present. We been hard upon the road since the night before, on account of a certain colonel who took exception to his new recruits drinking the professor's elixir and sent a squad of lively fellows to arrest us.

The professor bribed them with silver coin, but still we had to flee and put many miles behind us before the sun rose.

I'm riding in the third wagon with Tally, trying to persuade him to stop and cook us breakfast.

"They say an army travels on its stomach," I remind him. "What about medicine shows? Don't we travel on our stomachs, too?"

Tally shakes his head, keeps the wagon moving. "I believe there's an old leather boot under the seat," he says. "Chew on that, if you like."

"What's that I hear?" I say, putting my hand to my ear.

"Distant thunder? Artillery? No—it's your empty belly! What a lonesome, hungry noise it makes. Pancakes, Tally. Fried potatoes. Strawberry pie."

"Strawberry pie?"

"We passed a whole field of strawberries, not a mile back. Fresh strawberries baked in a pie. Mmmmm, good," I say, taunting him by rubbing my stomach.

"Stop it, you little scamp! We'll have our breakfast when the professor says so, and not before."

That's when the great black monster comes over the horizon, blown by the warm summer wind. Looks like a giant head making faces at us as it rises over the grassy hills.

"Professor!" Tally cries, standing up in his seat. "Look!"

The wagons halt as an enormous silk balloon fills the sky. The silk bulges and ripples, changing shape with the wind, and looks like a thing alive.

As it gets closer I can make out a basket hanging by ropes, and a man in the basket, waving frantically and pointing at something. Beneath the basket is another long rope dragging an anchor. The anchor keeps hitting the ground and bouncing back up in the air.

"Runaway balloon," Tally says, his eyes lighting up. "Bernard! Let's grab the anchor!"

The juggling brothers leap from their wagons and give chase. I follow close behind, striving to keep up. The man shouts from the basket, but he must be a hundred feet in the air and the words are jumbled.

We're in a country of rolling hills, running through knee-high grass, chasing the anchor as it tumbles and bounces.

Tally gets his hand on the anchor and gives a yell of triumph, and then he's yanked into the air and falls, tumbling head over heels in the soft grass.

Next thing, Bern leaps over his fallen brother and snatches at the anchor. It drags him along and spins him around as the great balloon pops up again, pushed by the wind.

"Grab my legs!" he yells.

Somehow I manage to get both arms around his legs. For a moment the extra weight seems to hold us down, with my toes dragging along in the grass. Then another gust lifts us high into the air and we're both screaming for help.

Far below us Tally is running to keep up, begging us to come down to earth. We would if we could, but the fall is too far. I'm hanging on to Bern's legs for dear life. Then as the hill below us rises to the ridge, we swing closer to the ground.

We're going so fast the grass looks blurry.

"Look out!" Tally yells, pointing.

At the top of the hill looms a cluster of tall elm trees. We're heading right for it! The thick branches look like spears rushing at us. I've half a mind to drop and take my chances, but before I can figure out how to let go we swoosh into the trees.

Last thing I see is a branch exactly as fat as my head.

THE SMELL WAKES ME. The delicious smell of sausage cooking in a fry pan, and coffee boiling on an open fire.

Mini is holding a cool, damp cloth to my forehead, and she smiles when I wake up.

"Good thing your skull is so thick," she says. "It's pure luck your head didn't get cracked like an egg when it hit that tree. What were you thinking? That you could fly like a bird?"

Above us the giant balloon is tethered to the elm tree, bobbing to and fro in the breeze. The anchor has wrapped around the branches. The balloon looks so peaceful you'd never know that when it gets loose it has a mind to kill the people that are trying to help it.

"Glad to see you back in this world," Bern says, bending down to give my nose a tweak.

Bern got stove up some, mostly scratches, but he expects breakfast will revive him. Tally is busy cooking, using every available fry pan. Preparing sausage and eggs and fried potatoes and onions and what he calls his sure-fire pan-fried biscuits.

When he notices me sitting up, holding my swollen, achy head, he apologizes for not getting any strawberries.

"I was willing to go back," he says. "But the professor insisted we all stay with the balloon." Whispering, he adds, "I think he means to buy it!"

Sure enough, the professor is deep in conversation with the man who was riding in the basket. He's a young, slender, dandified fellow with a wispy black beard and a long skinny nose and the blazing eyes of a true believer.

"Aeronautics is the future!" he's telling the professor with great enthusiasm. "Thaddeus Lowe is the living proof! Nine hundred miles in nine hours!"

The young man, Mr. Dennett Bobbins by name, explains that Thaddeus Lowe was appointed by President Lincoln to be Chief of Army Aeronautics after Mr. Lowe flew a balloon from Cincinnati, Ohio, to Unionville, South Carolina, in the aforementioned nine hours. For a time his fleet of army airships flew over the northern part of Virginia, reporting on Confederate positions.

Lately, it seems, Confederate sharpshooters and artillery men have learned how to shoot down the balloons, which do make rather large targets.

"A thousand square yards of silk!" Mr. Bobbins raves. "Twenty-eight thousand cubic feet of hydrogen, generated on the battlefield! Ten thousand feet of cable to tether us in place! From ten thousand feet you can see to the ends of the earth, Tilda and I! The movements of the enemy lose all mystery! Armies can no longer rely upon surprise attacks! I tell you, aeronautics is the future! The future, I say!"

And then suddenly he commences to sob. Tears stream down his cheeks as Mr. Bobbins tells us that on account of so many unfortunate accidents — the unpredictable wind, the hydrogen gas catching afire — the entire aeronautical division is to be shut down. Mr. Bobbins's balloon is the last of the fleet and he has failed in his attempt to survey the Potomac valley and relay intelligence by telegraph to the ground.

"A summer storm!" he wails. "I saw a few thunderheads gathering, but gave the order to launch despite the threat of storms! It's my fault, not Tilda's! It was our last chance to prove the value of airships and I failed! I failed most miserably! Oh Tilda, do forgive me!"

As the young airship pilot weeps and wails, Professor Fleabottom pats him on the back and comforts him.

"It's not your fault, my good sir, you can't be responsible for the weather," he assures him.

After a time Mr. Bobbins calms down, accepts a tin mug of coffee from Minerva, and only then seems to take note of his surroundings. "Where am I, precisely?" he wants to know.

"In the general vicinity of Lancaster," the professor informs him.

"Lancaster! Indeed. Then according to my calculations, we covered less than fifty miles." He looks up at the balloon bobbing over the elm tree. "She's a good ship. With a will of her own, obviously."

"Tell us, please, of your great adventure," the professor says, sounding very kind and solicitous. "Were you able to survey the Potomac valley? Could you discern the Confederate positions? Were you able to pass useful intelligence to the Union generals?"

Young Mr. Bobbins sighs and shakes his head. "Alas, no. There were obscuring clouds and then, just as Tilda and I attained peak altitude, we broke loose from the cable. Disaster!"

"You keep referring to a woman named Tilda. Had you another companion along for the ride?"

Mr. Bobbins looks shocked at the question. "Another companion? No, no. The 'we' is Tilda and I. She is my only companion."

"The balloon?"

"The airship!"

"Of course. Yes, indeed, the airship. *Tilda* being the name of the airship," the professor concludes thoughtfully. "Mini, would you get Mr. Bobbins a plate of food? I fear his head may be somewhat light from lack of sustenance, or possibly oxygen. Ten thousand feet is very high indeed. The air must be terribly thin."

"Not so thin as to addle my brain, if that's what you're implying," Mr. Bobbins says, sounding hurt and angry.

"Nothing of the sort!" the professor assures him. "Men have always given female names to waterborne ships, why not to ships of the air? Makes perfect sense if you think about it. Tilda, yes, she's a lovely creature."

"She's not a creature, she's an airship!" Mr. Bobbins protests.

"Of course, an airship. Please take no offense at our ignorance, good sir. We are fascinated with the whole concept of airships, and how they might prove useful to our little traveling enterprise."

"Aeronautics will change the world!" Mr. Bobbins

exclaims, regaining his enthusiasm. "There will come a day when all of humanity travels by air. We must learn to control the wind! That's the secret! That's the answer! Once we control the wind, we control the world!"

"Windmills, I suppose?" the professor offers cautiously. "Is that how you will control the wind?"

The young pilot gives him a disappointed look. "You doubt me, but one day it will be true. Humanity will travel by air, and conduct war from the air, and seek peace in the air. The air is the future, not the land! Mankind must be made free! It must unshackle from the slavery of gravity and be free as the clouds, like Tilda and me. Air, do you hear me, air!"

Poor Mr. Bobbins is still raving when the cavalry charges over the hill to arrest us all for treason.

28

LIKE A SQUIRREL
UP A TREE

IN LESS TIME THAN IT takes to whistle "Yankee Doodle," we're surrounded by a squad of grim-faced soldiers on horseback, all of 'em pointing long rifles in our faces.

"Keep your hands in plain view!" one of them shouts. "Anybody moves they are done for!"

The captain dismounts from his horse. He's a tall, fine-looking fellow, taller even than Professor Fleabottom, with piercing dark eyes and a nose like a hawk. Like the hawk, he has the look of a dangerous creature, one who may attack without warning.

He adjusts the cuffs of his white leather gloves, then strides up to the campfire and demands a cup of coffee.

"Are these true coffee beans?" he wants to know, seizing a battered tin mug. "Or have you taken up the rebel habit of adding chicory?"

Tally, who is tending the fire, looks like he don't know what to do or say.

"Cat got your tongue?" the captain demands. "Or is it General Lee who has charge of your tongue?"

Tally glances helplessly at Professor Fleabottom, who gathers himself up and says, "We beg your kindness, captain. This man is simpleminded. Your sudden arrival has confused him."

The captain snorts and puts his hand upon the pistol holstered at his waist. "Simpleminded, is he? I doubt that. Maybe the recruiters fall for such nonsense, but not me."

"Please, you are welcome to coffee, or indeed to any food we may have," the professor says, sounding rather grand. "Would your men like biscuits and jam, sir? Our cook may be simple, but he makes a very fine biscuit. Or if you prefer, we have sufficient bottles of my, ah, special elixir."

The captain gulps down his coffee, spits some of it back, and drops the mug in the fire. Then he strides full up to the professor, so close they almost bump chests. "You'd addle the brains of my men with your moonshine whiskey?" he asks, very quiet. "Is that your plan of escape? Get us drunk and sneak away?"

"Elixir for what ails you," responds the professor, holding his ground.

"Whiskey!" roars the captain. "Cheap whiskey!"

Mini dabs a hankie to her eyes, weeping. Bern and Tally both look like they want to bolt, but don't dare for fear of getting a bullet in the back. Mr. Bobbins just looks confused, and me, I'm thinking when the shooting starts I'll climb the tree and hide in the branches like a squirrel.

The captain whips a folded piece of paper out of his jacket and reads from it. "Reginald Robertson Crockett, also known as Fenton J. Fleabottom, as the duly authorized representative of the United States of America, I place you under arrest for the felony crime of treason." Looking up from the paper, he adds, "The specific and mortal crime of passing military intelligence to the enemy. Seize him!"

Four soldiers grab the professor, one for each limb. Not that he's fighting them. The professor looks disappointed in the poor captain but he don't struggle as they slip irons around his wrists and ankles.

"My dear captain, there has been a mistake. I freely confess to selling elixir to the troops. You have me there, fair and square. I further admit that what I call 'elixir' is really whiskey with a little flavoring of red clover cough syrup. But never would I betray my country. Not for a million in gold!"

The captain narrows his hawk eyes, looking crafty. "I believe you, sir. That you would not willingly betray your country. You have that air about you. But the truth is, your country is the Confederacy, and therefore you are a spy and a traitor and will pay the price."

"That's a lie! Bring me a Bible and I will swear upon it!"

The captain smiles and leans in, his sharp little chin not an inch from the professor's yellow mustache. "I am not so easily persuaded. It is well known that men who swear lying oaths upon the Bible believe that God is on their side, and will protect them despite the lie. But God Almighty will not answer in this instance. We have you dead to rights, Mr. Crockett. You are well known in Virginia as a staunch advocate of the southern rebellion, and Union spy catchers have been on your trail for months."

The professor looks puzzled. "Crockett? Who is this Crockett you refer to? My name is Fleabottom. You have mistaken me for another man!"

"That is your defense? Mistaken identity?"

"My defense is that I am innocent," the professor protests. "What exactly is it that you think I have done?"

The captain stands back, readjusting his white leather gloves. "Do you deny that you have been making inquiries about the movement of troops?"

"Of course I deny it! An absurd idea. I'd never—oh, wait a moment! Oh, yes. That has to be it! I know what has happened, and why you have been deceived." The professor is smiling now, looking much relieved. "It's the boy! Over there, the small one cowering by the elm tree. Homer Figg by name. He's much concerned with finding his older brother, who was sworn as a replacement troop, and may be underage."

The captain turns and fixes me with his hungry, hawkish eyes. "Come here, boy!"

I shamble forward. The way he stares at me so hard and cold turns my stomach to water and makes my knees shaky.

"Is this true?" he demands. "Have you asked this man to help you find your brother?"

"Y-y-yes, sir."

"And this man, who calls himself Professor Fleabottom, he has on your behalf made many inquiries that touch upon Union troop movements? Interviewed and interrogated soldiers and officers after getting them drunk? All to help you find your brother?"

"Yes, sir. He's been very kind and helpful, sir."

"Indeed," says the captain, stroking his chin with the fingers of his white leather gloves. "No doubt he is kind when it suits him, that much I would not dispute."

"So you understand that this is simply an unfortunate misunderstanding," says the professor, holding out his wrists to be freed. "Such things readily occur in a time of war, captain. I assure you, there are no hard feelings on my part."

The captain snorts, amused by the professor. "Very good of you, sir. No doubt, being a Virginian, you are a man of courage and honor. You will have need of both when they drag you to the gallows."

"But, captain, surely you see that I was only trying to help the boy?"

The captain shrugs. "The boy was your excuse. The game is up, Mr. Crockett." He jabs a finger at one of his men. "Sergeant! Produce the prisoner!"

The horses make way for another horse, a pony that has been kept behind and out of sight.

A man has been tied facedown across the back of the pony. He appears alive but barely conscious, and shows the marks of a terrible beating. Both eyes blackened and his whole face swole up like an overripe melon, but still I recognize the mysterious rider who came into camp that night and took a dispatch from the professor.

The poor man must hurt in every bone of his body, but he don't make a sound.

Upon seeing the injured man, Professor Fleabottom heaves a sigh of defeat. His mustache droops and his shoulders sag, like somebody let the air out of him.

The captain says, "I see you do not deny your own brother, Mr. Levi Crockett, soon to be late of Richmond, Virginia. He was shadowed these past few months, as have you been, and was finally caught red-handed with your dispatch in his pack. The dispatch, describing Union positions in great detail, was written in your hand and seen to be delivered to your brother in the dead of night. On this there can be no dispute, and no excuse or clever lie will change that."

"Levi, I am sorry," the professor calls out, a catch in his great, booming voice.

The captain nods, satisfied. "The traitor's noose will soon be upon your necks. Make peace with your Maker, Mr. Crockett, and prepare to go to a better place."

"Murderers!" Mini screams, flinging a pot at the captain. "Killers!"

The pot lands harmlessly at the captain's feet. His eyes gleam like black pebbles at the bottom of a cold stream, and he seems very pleased with himself. "Arrest them all!"

he commands. "The tattooed harridan, the draft-dodging jugglers—and don't forget the boy!"

Before he gets to "boy" I'm up the tree and into the basket beneath the swaying balloon, fast as any squirrel and twice as scared.

Far below, at the base of the elm, a couple of the soldiers laugh and argue about who will climb the tree to claim me.

"Why he ain't much bigger than a pint of spit!" someone cackles, and they all laugh so hard they have to hold their bellies.

They never notice Tally's kitchen knife is missing, so the laugh is on them when I cut the anchor rope and make my escape in a giant silk balloon, made for the Union Army.

The last thing I hear before the wind carries me away is Mr. Bobbins screaming for his Tilda.

29

LIKE A BIRD WITH
A BROKEN WING

UNTIL THAT FATEFUL BALLOON ride, the highest I ever been was to the peak of Squint's hay barn. I was five or six years old and somehow got it in mind to see the world, or maybe to catch one of the pigeons that hopped along the ridge. Truth is, I don't recall exactly what was in my head at the time, all I remember is Harold in the yard below, pleading for me to come down, and how it amused me to hear him begging.

It was a mean thing, wanting to scare my big brother, who had always been so kind to me. But it felt good, too, like I enjoyed testing how much he loved me. Eventually I came down on my own, none the worse for wear, and Harold swore if I ever did such a thing again — climb that rickety old roof like a monkey — he'd kill me with his own hands, but I knew he didn't mean it, and that made me feel good, too.

I mention this because I scampered into that balloon with nothing in my head but the desire to get away, and no idea what it meant to cut the anchor line. I wasn't thinking about how you get down again, that's for sure.

Without the weight of the anchor the balloon shoots straight up into the sky, rising so fast it leaves my stomach back there in the elm tree. It's like being on a rocket without the sparkles. By the time I dare to peek over the side of the basket, the ground is already falling away. Professor Fleabottom and the others are no bigger than tiny little ants and getting smaller fast.

I'm heading up to Heaven with no way back.

All of a sudden the wind howls like a shrieking bird, making the balloon sway violently. The basket thrashes up, down, and sideways. One second I'm screaming into the wind, directly under the balloon, the next I'm looking straight down at the ground, clinging to the basket with all my fingers and every last toe.

I hang on for dear life—a giant balloon named Tilda wants to cough me out like a fur ball from a sick cat!

About the time my heart is fixing to stop, the basket swings back under the balloon and holds steady, more or less. Gives me a chance to catch my breath in the thin air, and to realize that not all the shivering comes from being afraid—the closer you get to Heaven, the colder it gets.

With things settled down for the time being, I search around the bottom of the basket, looking for something useful. The kitchen knife has fallen away, but lashed to the framework of the basket is a canteen of water and a packet of hardtack biscuits. Not that I'm hungry — you need a stomach to be hungry, and mine got left behind.

After a while, a hundred years or so, I find the courage to peek over the side.

Big mistake. This high up you can't see people or animals, and the cornfields look like ragged green patches on a big old quilt. Train tracks are like stitches in the ground, mending the world together. Beyond the forests and the fields and villages that look like toys, and the snaky silver rivers glinting in the sun, the great curved edge of the earth blends into the sky.

That's where Heaven and earth must meet, in a haze of blue mist at the far end of the world.

———

I FLY FOR HOURS IT SEEMS, and going west we chase the sun, the great balloon and I, as if to make the day last longer. You get used to anything, I suppose, even flying high above the earth, and after a while it comes to feel natural. Almost like I belong in the air, floating higher than birds can fly.

Looking out over the world, it feels like I'm more than a runaway orphan boy, like I'm bigger than Homer Figg from Pine Swamp, Maine. Like I've somehow become everybody that ever lived, and we're all of us watching over the earth like a mother hen watching over her egg.

Which is a pretty crazy way to think. How could I be everybody that ever lived when I'm just one small person? Must be the thin air putting wild thoughts in my head, or fumes from the great balloon. Speaking of the balloon, it keeps changing shape, very gently. Shaped by the wind, I suppose, but it almost looks like it's breathing. Little ripples move along the surface like waves in a silk pond, and if you stare hard enough there's a face in the balloon just like there's a face in the moon or clouds. A face that keeps changing and growing the longer you look. A face that's trying to tell me something important.

Tilda is talking to me, only I can't hear the words.

Then I realize that what looks like a smiling mouth in the balloon face is really a tear in the silk.

A tear in the silk that's flapping as the gas escapes.

I been staring at the balloon so long, daydreaming about faces and clouds and such, that I forgot to look down. And when I do, peering fearfully over the edge of the basket, the ground is coming up fast.

We're falling from the sky like a bird with a broken wing.

30

WHEN THE SCREAMING
COMES INSIDE

As we drop closer to the ground everything speeds up. It's like the earth is turning faster, whipping great trees at the basket and barely missing. Then we're flying over rocky fields, Tilda and me, fields where men on horseback chase one another, firing guns and waving swords. Suddenly the ground explodes under the horses, and man and beast vanish in a flash of blood-stained lightning.

We're being swept over a battlefield, and what I thought was thunder and lightning is artillery shells blowing the world to pieces.

Right about then the rip in the silk catches fire and the fabric starts to melt. I scramble over the side of the basket, clinging with my fingers, deciding when to jump. All I catch is a glimpse of green water, but with the balloon dissolving into red-hot flames, making up my mind is no longer an option. I must let go and take my chances.

I drop through the air like a screaming stone, plunging feet first into a scummy green frog pond.

When you're falling from a hundred feet or more, and the sky is on fire, even scummy water is better than solid ground. At least the fall don't kill me. Trouble is, I can't find the surface. Can't tell which way is up because my fists are full of mud, like I been clawing at the bottom, and my legs are caught in a tangle of lily pad roots that want to tug me down.

I'm trying to breathe the warm, slimy water — if frogs can do it, why not me? — when something grabs hold of my hair and yanks me up into the sunlight.

Can't see right off, because I'm coughing so hard, but after a few minutes of having the water shook out of me, I realize I been saved by a scrawny little man in a gray uniform. He's missing his front teeth and his tongue keeps sliding over the gap as he shakes me. Then he hands me over to a bunch of men in gray uniforms, that have been refreshing their horses at the edge of the pond.

Cavalry, from the look. They talk funny, kind of slow and lilting, but I can understand them well enough.

"Little critter fell out of the sky, did he?"

"Yes, suh, like he'd been shot from a cannon."

"Weren't no cannon, suh! He come by way of surveillance balloon. That's what's left of it, burning in those trees over yonder."

"Is that a fact?"

"Yes, suh!"

"Must be a Yankee spy, getting a fix on our position."

"Suh, he ain't but a boy!"

Another, more powerful voice cuts through the argument. "What have we here? Report!"

Rough hands pass me along to where a beautifully uniformed man sits on horseback, hands folded over the pommel. Looks like he lives in the saddle and likes it there. He wears an elegant cape and a rakish hat decorated with a long plumed feather. A fancy sword hangs from his waist.

"Yankee boy fell out of a balloon, General Jeb, suh!"

The dashing young general leans down from the saddle to study me. Makes a show of tugging at his thick, full beard. "Hmmm. Might be a boy," he drawls, a twinkle in his eyes. "And might be he's a midget spy, dressed to look like a boy. I wouldn't put it past them clever Yankees to fool us with midgets and what not."

"Yes, suh!"

The men are grinning, as if they know their general likes to make jokes.

"What's your name, midget man?" the general demands. "I've miles to ride and haven't the time or stomach for any more tomfoolery. Tell me your name!"

"H-h-homer Figg. And I ain't no midget!"

"Yankee for sure. Take him to the bull pit!"

———

Turns out a bull pit is where prisoners get confined, and in this case the pit is a stall in an old barn that's been temporarily requisitioned by the Confederate forces who stand guard outside — *requisitioned* being another word for "stole," which is what armies do when they need things.

All of which is explained to me by a bright young fellow named Jonathan Griswold, who says he is correspondent for the *Valley Spirit*, a newspaper in Chambersburg.

"I should be in the office, setting type," he explains, "but our fine little city has lately been overrun by invading rebels. They requisitioned all of the bread and grain, and every spare saddle, and all the horseshoes, and nails for the horseshoes, and looked about ready to requisition the printing press and me. Seemed a good opportunity to venture out and see the war!"

Mr. Jonathan Griswold has a mousey brown mustache, a pair of reading spectacles hanging from a ribbon around his skinny neck, and a whole cavalry of ideas and opinions at his command.

He says, "I rode out from a little town called Gettysburg, expecting to find the Union Army, and was intercepted by Stuart's raiders, who have no particular affection for Yankee newspapermen. I take it you were seized by the same fellows?"

"The man had a feather in his hat."

"Jeb Stuart himself!" the newspaperman says, sounding impressed. "They say he can ride circles around the Union Army, and will report back to Robert E. Lee before the main battle starts."

"He called me a midget!" I complain, still incensed. "A midget and a spy!"

The newspaperman chuckles. "Did he now? They've taken away my notebook but I must remember that. 'A midget and a spy.' That's an improvement on tales about girls who disguise themselves as soldiers, and dogs who save their masters. I can see you are no midget, sir. But if, as they tell me, you arrived by surveillance balloon, then surely you really are a spy of sorts? And too young for hanging, lucky for you."

Outside the stall the Confederate guards are acting ever so casual, smoking their pipes and complaining about the rations, but I can tell they're keeping keen ears for our conversation. So I decide to tell the newspaperman all about traveling with Professor Fleabottom, and that he's really a rebel patriot arrested by the Union Army, and how I escaped in a stolen balloon.

"Said his true name is Crockett, Reginald Robert Crockett," I say as my tale concludes. "He's got a brother, Levi, they beat up something awful."

"Crockett you say!" the newspaperman exclaims. "That's a famous name in the South. Was your medicine showman related to Davy Crockett, that died at the Alamo?"

"Must have been," I say, working up some enthusiasm for the idea. "In fact, I'm sure he is. I once saw him kill a mountain lion with his bare hands. Must be the Crockett blood."

"A mountain lion. Extraordinary! Bare hands, you say?"

"Course it was an old lion, missing most of its teeth. Escaped from a circus."

"And you were employed by Mr. Crockett, also known as Professor Fleabottom?"

"You might say so," I say grandly. "I was the star of the show."

"Star of the show? In what capacity?"

"I played the Amazing, um, the Amazing Wolf Boy. Raised by wolves and so on."

The newspaperman is nodding feverishly, as if anxious to write it down, if only he had pen and paper. The Confederate guards lean closer, hanging on my every word, just as I planned.

"Course I wasn't really raised by wolves," I confide. "I'm a Figg. You probably heard of the Figgs. We're the richest family north of Boston. Figgs own most of the timber, a railroad, a good portion of the mines, and a fleet of schooners. Plus too many farms and factories to bother mentioning. Why we even own slaves," I add, eyeing the guards. "Dozens of 'em. Hundreds, probably, if you took the trouble to count. We Figgs favor slavery. My father, when he was governor, he wrote a law saying every man must own a slave. Owning slaves is what makes America great, everybody knows that. Everybody but that fool Lincoln. My father says if Lincoln was to take away our slaves he'd chop old Abe down like Washington chopped down the cherry tree."

"Would he really?" asks the newspaperman, looking aghast.

"Course he would! Give up our slaves? Never! It's slaves that make us rich. Slaves that make us happy. Slaves that make the pancakes, and churn the butter, and boil the syrup. My father once give me a slave whose job it was to follow me around and sweep away my footprints so I could pretend to be invisible. That's how many slaves we owned, that he could spare one for erasing footprints."

"I see," says the newspaperman doubtfully.

"Point is, we Figgs may be from Maine, but our hearts lie with the Southern rebels. Yes, sir. Never met a slave I didn't want to own! Fact is, most every slave I ever saw we *did* own."

"Hundreds of them, you say. In Maine? With your, um, wealthy family?"

"Not wealthy—rich! Rich is better. More slaves if you're rich."

The Confederate guards are nodding at one another and one of them turns to leave. I figure he's off to tell his boss they have put a true friend of the South in jail by mistake.

That's when the screaming starts and ruins my plan. A terrible screaming that puts a chill down my spine and makes my knees shiver. A screaming that makes the guards forget the amazing story of the boy in the balloon.

"What's that?" I ask the newspaperman, whose face has gone gray.

"I think I know," he says. He pulls himself up to the barred window in one corner of the stall and has a look. He drops back down and wipes his sweaty hands on his trouser legs. "The wounded," he explains. "The battle must have begun. They're bringing wounded to the barn."

And then the doors burst open and the screaming comes inside.

31

ON THE TERRIBLE
FIRST DAY OF JULY

THEY COME BY THE CARTLOAD. Moaning soldiers
stacked in flatbed wagons or carts drawn by horse or by
hand. Mostly the wounded scream only when the cart hits
a bump. Some have already stopped screaming and are put
aside as the carts are unloaded, their faces covered with a
scrap of cloth.

The rest are carried into the barn on litters, awaiting
treatment. Dozens and dozens of men, some of them crying out for their mothers, wives, or their sweethearts. The
dozens soon become a hundred, stacked inside the barn and
out, under the shade of the eaves.

"The battle of Gettysburg has begun," the newspaperman confides. "They say that for part of the day the Union
cavalry held its own, but are now being driven back through
the town. According to our guard, thousands of Union
troops have surrendered or been taken prisoner. The reb-

els expect that Lincoln's army will be defeated in a day or two, just as they were at Chancellorsville, and then General Robert E. Lee and his troops will invade Washington from the north and declare victory."

"Is it true?" I want to know. "The North has lost?"

"Truth?" the newspaperman says, shaking his head. "The truth is hard to come by when the bullets are flying. The battle won't be truly won or lost until the dead are counted."

The rebels may be winning at Gettysburg, but their triumph is not without cost. Most of the wounded have been gravely injured and the rebel surgeons are as busy as carpenters, prying out bullets and sawing off limbs.

The only thing worse than a man screaming in pain is the sound of the saws cutting through bone.

"A good surgeon is like a good butcher—he knows his cut of meat. He will roll up his sleeves, administer a little ether if he's got it, and have a leg off and the stump cauterized in a few minutes," the newspaperman explains. "Longer than that and the man will die of pain, or loss of blood, or both. As it is, less than half of these men will survive the day. Of those that do, another half will die of infection."

Then I don't hear no more of what he's got to say because I'm covering my ears to muffle the screaming and the terrible wet noise of the saw. I curl up facing the wall so's not to watch the horrible business of tending to the wounded. Inside my head I'm praying Harold has not "seen the elephant" or been injured or worse. Best thing might be if he surrendered or was taken prisoner. But that's foolishness—a boy brave enough to stand up to Squinton Leach would never surrender to no rebel. Knowing Harold he's probably been promoted on the battlefield. Heck, if I don't find him soon he'll likely be the youngest general in history.

That's what I cling to: the thought of Harold somehow surviving. A fever dream of hope that I'll find him before he's killed and we'll escape back to Maine and kindly Mr. Brewster will take us in, and we'll live like proper people with beds to sleep in and three squares a day and milk and pie in the evenings. We'll sit by the fire, jawing with Mr. Brewster, and help the escaped slaves if they still need help, and make sure Bob the horse has plenty of hay, and oats if he wants them. I'll go to school like our Dear Mother intended and learn everything there is to know about the world. I'll learn how to stop people from starving, and put an end to wars and slavery and meanness and cruelty, and Harold will manage the tourmaline mines for Mr. Brewster. In my dream Harold will be happy and strong and find him a wife to darn his socks of an evening and give him children that are never hungry and never get beat or locked in the barn like animals, and never have to run away to war to save their big brothers and see arms and legs being stacked like cordwood, or men dying of their wounds, or hear the keening of boys who miss their mothers and beg to see her in Heaven.

They say that even in the worst battles some of the troops survive. Please, Dear Lord, let that someone be my big brother, that's all I'm asking. Don't let him die in a pony cart jammed with the wounded, or tied to a plank while they saw his limbs off, one by one, or carried home in a casket wagon.

Please, Dear Lord, please let him be okay, wherever he is, and tell him Homer is coming.

⌣

ALONG ABOUT NOON something changes. The cartloads of wounded stop arriving, and the pitiful moaning slacks off, and the weary surgeons and their assistants wash the blood from their hands and have something to eat and drink.

The horses and ponies that survived the battle are fed and watered, too, and some of them are put into stalls next to me and Jonathan Griswold, the newspaperman, where they neigh and nicker and rub themselves nervously against the stalls, as if trying to scratch away the fright of what they've been through.

"History is happening today," the newspaperman laments, fiddling with his spectacles. "And I am stuck in a barn with the dumb animals, blind as a bat. I've not even pen and ink to mark down rumors of these great events!"

"At least you have a hand to write with, even if you ain't got a pen," I remind him.

"True enough," he admits. "I should count my blessings."

There is triumphant talk among the troops that the war

has finally been won, that the Confederate troops will soon sweep away the last of the Union Army, and either kill them or take them prisoner.

The newspaperman, keeping his voice low, confides that it may be just as they say, but that the rebels have been chasing victory for two years and have never quite gotten there. He says that while each man the South loses is gone forever, the more populous North has more men to lose, and many more that can be drafted to replace them.

"In the end it is a game of numbers. Not so much who has the will to win, but who has the most men and material to sacrifice. The war is a meat grinder, as you have seen."

Sometime in the middle of the afternoon a messenger arrives, shouting at the top of his lungs.

"To the front! All men fit for fighting are commanded to the front! The Union Army flees and General Lee orders all fit men to the chase! Have at 'em, boys! We got 'em on the run at last!"

The barn is suddenly alive with cries for victory. Even some of the most desperate wounded beg to be taken back into battle, with rifles placed in their shivering hands.

"All men to the front! All men to the front! Long live the South! Long live Robert E. Lee!"

The men guarding us have been affected by the excitement. They pick up their weapons and haversacks and race from the barn to join their comrades, leaving me and the newspaperman pretty much alone.

"Now is our chance," I whisper. "I'll take the smallest horse."

He firmly shakes his head. "I dare not," he says, sounding regretful. "They will shoot me for certain."

"Will they shoot a boy?" I ask.

He shrugs. "Who can say what men will do when the heat of battle is upon them? But these rebels are decent enough. They will be aiming for men in blue uniforms." He looks at me with great concern. "But why flee? I thought you favored the South, that your family owned slaves by the dozen."

"By the hundreds," I tell him. "All lies. The only side I favor is named Harold Figg, and I will find him or die trying."

"There's an excellent chance you will succeed in dying," he warns me. "Best stay here and keep your head down."

"I made a promise," I explain. "Remember my name in case I am forgot. Homer Figg, of Pine Swamp, Maine."

A moment later I'm over the stall and leading a pony to daylight.

32

THINGS
BEST FORGOT

I LIKE TO BELIEVE THAT our Dear Mother watched over me that day. Maybe it is wishful to think that them in Heaven are concerned with those of us on earth, but *something* kept me alive, because by rights I should have been killed six times over.

The first is a hail of bullets zinging past my ears as I put heels to that rebel pony and gallop out of the farmyard. No saddle nor bridle to steer by, just me clinging to the mane for dear life, and bullets cleaving the air like invisible knives.

The next is not a mile away, when an artillery shell lands so close I can feel the heat as it explodes and smell the dirt in the air. Then I'm galloping the stolen pony through clouds of smoke, over rolling fields, over a railroad track, past thousands of soldiers massed to attack, and rolling batteries of artillery cannon, and startled men who shake their heads as me and the pony fly by, running for our lives.

Somehow the poor animal seems to understand that I want to go through the gray Confederate lines and head for the Union blue. Or maybe it's just so spooked that it runs straight at what frightens it most.

Time and again shells explode, tearing up the ground, knocking down trees, and making soldiers vanish, leaving nothing behind but their boots.

I cling to the pony as if in a bad dream, although it is nothing like the war in my nightmares, where I have seen Harold die a hundred times. In nightmares the noise of war is not louder than a thousand thunderstorms, or as blinding as a thousand bolts of lightning. In nightmares it never smelled so bad. In nightmares I do not hear the cry of wounded horses and think that it is worse than the cry-ing of wounded men because the animals do not understand what has happened to them, or why they have been shot down.

Men and horses are dying all around me and yet on I ride, on and on and on, spurring the pony with my bare heels, expecting to be struck at any moment.

Like the pony, fear keeps me going. That, and anger at being so scared. I keep riding and riding through bullets and bombshells because I am furiously afraid to stop mov-ing. Stopping is where the world explodes. Stopping is cer-tain death.

In that mad ride across the field of battle I see many things:

ARTILLERY SHELLS SKIPPING ALONG THE GROUND
LIKE ROCKS BEING SKIPPED ON A POND.

A CAVALRY OFFICER DRAWING HIS PISTOL
TO PUT DOWN HIS WOUNDED HORSE,
AND THEN HIMSELF FALLING LIFELESS BEFORE
HE CAN PULL THE TRIGGER.

MEN DIGGING LIKE DOGS IN THE DIRT TO GET AWAY
FROM THE DEADLY HAIL OF LEAD.

SPENT BULLETS SPATTERING LIKE HARD RAIN
ON THE BROKEN GROUND.

TREES BURNING LIKE CHRISTMAS CANDLES.

THIRSTY MEN SUCKING SWEAT FROM
THEIR WOOLEN SLEEVES.

A DEAD MAN ON HIS KNEES WITH HIS HANDS FOLDED,
AS IF TO PRAY.

THINGS TOO TERRIBLE TO WRITE, FOR FEAR
THE PAGE WILL BURN.

THINGS BEST FORGOT.

LATER SOMEONE TOLD ME I must have covered five miles or more, from the rebel-held farmhouse to the Union lines at Culp's Hill. To me it felt longer than forever. After a while I could not hear the fearsome thumping of the artillery, or the bee buzz of the bullets, or the crying of man and beast. It's as if my ears have been stuffed with thick cotton, muffling the noise of war. The only thing I can really be sure of is my own heart slamming, and the beating heart of the pony as we ride on through the carnage, leaping over the dead and dying, our pace never slacking.

It's as if me and the pony exist all to ourselves, inside the battle but somehow separate. Galloping on and on until suddenly the smoke clears away and there's a sloping hill in front of us and rows and rows of cannons pointing their dark black barrels right at me, speaking in puffs of white smoke, and I'm shouting back at the cannons, shouting for my brother, but I can't hear my own voice.

The pony rears up and I lose my hold, falling with a hard thump to the rocky ground. Can't tell if I'm seeing stars, or real shells exploding, and then rough hands grab me and pull me into a trench dug in the ground below the cannon.

Bearded men in blue uniforms are shouting, but I can't make out what they're saying. Finally one of them gives me water and covers my ears with a cool damp cloth and slowly my hearing returns.

"Who are you, boy? Have you lost your mind? Charging

over a battlefield without so much as a sword or gun? That's madness! Four or five of our best sharpshooters were trying to cut you down, I don't know how they missed!"

"Are you from Maine?" I ask, gulping the water.

"Vermont," says the man with the water. "Poultney, Vermont. I never been to Maine, nor anywhere else but here."

I try to explain about my brother, that he will be with a company of new recruits from Maine, but the Vermont man has no patience for my story.

"Medicine shows? Pigs like human beings? Confederate spies? Balloon rides? You're speaking nonsense, boy! You took a bad fall and it's gone to your head!"

"Harold Figg," I insist. "He's not yet eighteen!"

The Vermont man shrugs. "There are drummer boys of fourteen or even younger. Drummer boys no older than you!"

"He was sworn to fight as a soldier," I try to explain, but the cannons fire directly over our heads and once again my ears go deaf for a time.

When the cannons are reloading for another salvo, the Vermont man hauls me over the top of the hill, out of the line of fire, and won't let me go until he's delivered me to his company sergeant.

"This boy was recovered on the field of battle!" he yells to a sergeant. "He's plum crazy! What should I do?"

"Send him to the rear!" shouts the sergeant, pointing with his sword. "All civilians to the rear! And be quick about it, private! The Johnny Rebs are coming again, sure as Christmas. They will mount one last assault before the sun sets!"

There are thousands of soldiers upon the hill and just behind it, and from the look most have been fighting all day. The wounded are being loaded into wagons and will be carried to where the Union surgeons await.

Just over the ridge the cannons are booming, but here there are fires lit, and camp stoves where coffee brews, and the men all seem calm and tired but also full of purpose.

"They have seen the worst of war and are determined to keep fighting," the Vermont man says, with great satisfaction. "We stand our ground at last."

He fetches a mug of hot black coffee and bids me drink it. "Might be this'll restore your sanity," he says. "It must suffice, for I can't be babysitting a lunatic boy. I must return to my men before the next assault, or be marked down as a deserter."

"Thank you," I say. "I'm fine now. It was all the noise made my head crooked."

"It'll do that," he agrees, and points to the wagons. "Best thing, follow the wounded. That will get you a safe distance from the fighting. Don't know what became of your little horse. I think it may still be running."

I promise to follow the wagons of wounded and find safety in the rear, but as soon as he's out of sight I skedaddle to another group of soldiers, asking if any are from Maine.

None are—they're all Pennsylvania volunteers, and some from New York, and they know nothing of the regiments from Maine, or where they might be located.

Before they can ask what a boy is doing on the battlefield, out of uniform, I move on to the next group, looking for my brother. Fact is, they're all too busy to take much notice of me, or too tired to give chase.

As the sun is going down, I finally come upon some men from Maine, and ask if they have any Figgs along.

"Figs, son? Figs?" says one of the soldiers, grinning so hard his droopy mustache goes horizontal. "How about apples or peaches? Would you settle for a pear? We have a Private Charles Pear, from Brunswick."

"Figg," I insist. "Harold Figg, from Pine Swamp."

"Never heard of Pine Swamp. Never heard of Harold Figg. Do you know what regiment? What division?"

"All I know is, he's my brother and he's in the army."

"And how did you come to be here, boy, looking for your brother?"

I'm too exhausted to tell the story again, with or without the ornamentation. "I come by train," I tell him, to keep it simple.

"All the way to Gettysburg by train?"

"The last stretch by horse," I admit.

The soldier studies me in the fading light. "You look like you could use a meal, son. Why not join us? We are all Maine men here, though none called Figg."

"I must find my brother," I insist.

"Night falls," he warns. "If you wander in the wrong direction the pickets will shoot you. Can't find your brother if you're shot, can you?"

"No, sir."

"Then join us for a little while," he suggests. "Our cook is making soup in that big iron pot. A fine potato soup that we pretend is fish chowder. You can look for your brother tomorrow, at first light. If his company is within marching distance they'll be on the move, coming our way. All companies have been summoned to Gettysburg. One way or another he'll be in the fight. Tomorrow, son, that's when you'll find him."

I figure to have a little of that fine-smelling potato soup and then move along, keep looking. I settle down by the fire, spooning the soup out of a tin pan — tastes as good as it smells — and then another soldier gives me his ration of hardtack and shows me how to soak it in the soup and I eat that, too. Then when I'm about ready to set out again, dark or not, the regimental band decides to play, and it seems impolite to sneak away, especially with so many familiar Maine voices raised in song:

The Union forever! Hurrah, boys, hurrah!

Down with the traitors, up with the stars;

While we rally 'round the flag, boys, rally once again,

Shouting the battle cry of freedom!

Later on, as my eyelids grow heavy, a young soldier with a fine high tenor sings "Just Before the Battle, Mother," a sad song about a boy telling his Dear Mother not to worry, and that's what carries me off to sleep, dreaming of mothers and brothers and sons.

33

"M IS FOR MUTINEER"

JUST BEFORE DAWN I AM awakened by a tall, skinny soldier who finds me sleeping near the smoldering campfire.

"Is it really you?" he asks, prodding my shoulder. "Is it really Homer Figg? They said a boy named Figg."

At first I do not recognize him, so changed is he.

"It's me, Webster B. Willow," he says. "Formerly a clergyman. Formerly acting on behalf of your guardian, Mr. Brewster. Formerly robbed and abandoned by the beautiful Kate Nibbly and her so-called brother. Now enlisted for my sins as Private Willow of the Fifth Maine, and come to beg for your forgiveness in case I am killed in the fighting."

He removes his forage cap and looks at the ground, as if ashamed to meet my eyes.

"It is I who was robbed and abandoned," I remind him, sitting up.

He nods miserably. "You tried to warn me but I was a fool. Still am a fool, no doubt. Mr. Brewster trusted me to look after you and I failed to do so."

"How long were you married?"

He shudders. "A few hours. Long enough to know I had been duped. Frank and Kate vanished as soon as we departed the ship. I searched for them on Park Avenue. Presented myself at the Nibbly mansion, like a fool, still hoping we had been separated by accident, and was told enough to glean the truth. Their real name, whatever it is, cannot be Nibbly."

"How did you find me?" I ask, still a little groggy from sleep.

"Someone mentioned a boy named Figg, searching for his brother. To be truthful, I debated most of the night whether or not I should make myself known to you."

"I still ain't found Harold."

Private Willow shifts uncomfortably and clears his skinny throat. "That's the other thing I have to tell you. After I was mustered in New York, joining this regiment, I briefly met another new recruit named Harold Figg. We were on the same troop train for part of a journey. He looks a lot like you, but larger, of course—I recognized him at a glance."

"You met my brother? Where is he? Did you say I was coming to get him?"

Private Willow shakes his head in misery. "I, um, I failed

to confess to him my association with you. Out of shame and despair."

"I don't care about that!" I say, leaping to my feet. "Where's Harold?"

Private Willow finally looks me in the eye. "He is with Colonel Chamberlain's men. The Twentieth Maine. They are marching from Hanover and should be here in a few hours time."

It takes a moment for me to understand what he's saying. "So Harold wasn't in Gettysburg yesterday when it all started? He ain't been in the battle yet? He ain't been wounded or killed?"

Private Willow puts on his forage cap and sets it straight. He shoulders his rifle and throws his narrow shoulders back, as if at attention. "I cannot say how your brother fares, young sir, but his regiment has not yet joined the battle. They must do so today. Today we all fight, every last man of us. The Johnny Rebs will do the same. Many thousands are sure to die."

"Are you afraid?" I ask.

He hesitates. "Not as much as I was, having spoken to you. But mighty fearful just the same."

I take Private Willow's hand and give it a quick squeeze. "I have seen the elephant and you got nothing to be feared of," I tell him.

That's a lie, but I owed him one, and hopeful lies don't count as bad.

THANKS TO PRIVATE WILLOW, when the 20th Maine Infantry Regiment comes marching into Gettysburg, I'm there at the Hanover Road, waiting to greet them.

They come along at a brisk march, three hundred and fifty men with a drum and fife keeping time as they kick up the dust. They've been on the road for hours and look tired but determined. Some raise cheers, anxious to join the fight.

Searching for my brother's face among them, I'm thinking all of my adventures have been worth it because I got here in time to stop Harold dying in battle. Surely he will be amazed to see me, and want to know how his little brother beat him to the war.

"Harold!" I cry. "Harold Figg!"

There's a fearsome-looking sergeant carrying the regiment flag, holding it high and proud. He tries to ignore me, but after the men are told to be "at ease," he plants the flag in the ground and crosses his big arms and gives me a stern look. "What do you want, boy? Don't you know this is a war? Go on home to your mother!"

"I want to see my brother, Harold Figg!" I insist. "He started out as a private but it's certain he's been promoted by now."

The sergeant gets a look on his face like he's swallowed a bad egg. He spits prodigiously and snarls, "Harold Figg, bah! He's been promoted all right. Promoted to the rear!"

"Promoted to corporal? Or is it colonel?"

"He's in irons, you young fool!" the sergeant roars. "Arrested and under guard! Now be off, afore the fighting starts! Away with you!"

Harold arrested? I assume the burly sergeant is having a joke at my expense. A bad, cruel joke. But when I go around to the back of the regiment, where some rickety wagons and a few horses have been brought up to join the fight, another soldier tells me that if I want to see Private Harold Figg I will have to parlay with the guards.

In one of the wagons, under guard of three armed soldiers, are five or six prisoners, each with a large, crude *M* chalked upon his blue uniform.

"*M* is for mutineer," a guard tells me, showing me his piece of chalk. "That's my idea. The *M* will be something to aim at if they try running away, ha-ha."

The guard's laughter is cruel, as if he thinks he's made a funny joke and doesn't care who it hurts.

One of the prisoners, a scurvy-looking fellow with a black eye, is my brother, Harold. When I call his name he covers his face and weeps.

34

ONE SMALL
HILL

ALL MY LIFE, I NEVER KNEW Harold to be scared or ashamed, and seeing him this way is like stepping backward off a cliff. Or discovering the world has gone inside out and upside down. I sit next to where he crouches in the wagon and try not to look at his black eye, or notice the sickly unwashed smell of him.

"Homer, what are you doing here?" he asks, his voice catching.

"Thought I'd take a stroll behind the barn and this is where I ended up." I give him a playful nudge. "I come looking for you, silly! To tell you it was nothing but a trick, making you enlist in the army. Squint sold you for a substitute and kept the money. They fooled you into enlisting. It ain't legal."

Harold hangs his head. His voice is so small I have to lean in close. "Don't matter now, Homer. I went and done it and will be court-martialed."

"What happened?" I ask. "Did you run from the bullets? Did you run from the cannon? From men with bayonets?"

My brother shakes his head. Somewhere in all his sorrow there comes a slight chuckle. "Disobeyed my squad sergeant. I swear he's worse than Squint."

"Is that what happened to your eye?"

He nods. "At first I liked it, being in the regiment. The fine uniform and the drilling. Shooting rifles. Three good meals a day. Sleeping in tents. I even like the marching, and folks cheering as we went by. But I never did like the sergeant telling me what to do without so much as a 'please' or 'thank you,' and one day I told him so. When he objected I slung him down in the mud, just like I did to Squint. It got worse from there," he adds. "He took it upon himself to make my life a misery. Said I was swamp trash not fit to serve."

"So you ran away?"

"Didn't get far, as you can see."

"What will happen?"

"It doesn't matter, little brother. I am disgraced. You must leave here and forget you ever knew me."

"Don't be stupid. That sergeant has knocked the sense right out of you."

"I mean it, Homer. You need to get away from here! Whatever happened yesterday, whatever you might have seen, it's nothing to what will happen today and tomorrow, and every day until one side or the other is defeated."

"Couldn't be worse than yesterday," I tell him.

"Oh yes, it could! The Union has ninety thousand men and will use them all. The rebels a similar number. Can't you hear the artillery pounding away? It has started already."

"It ain't fair," I say.

"Fair doesn't signify. I swore an oath and disobeyed. I must be punished."

"Do they hang mutineers?"

"Sometimes. Mostly not. Likely they'll send me to prison."

Up to now I've been trying to act cheerful, pretending things ain't so bad. But the prospect of Harold being sent off to prison in disgrace makes me gloomy and quiet. Probably they won't let me go off to prison with him. I'll have to visit, and smuggle in a saw so he can make his escape. Then we'll run away, as far as we can get. As far as the Western Territories, maybe, where land is free and nobody cares what happened in the war. We'll grow so much corn that we'll get fat as ticks, and build us a fine house with a fireplace and windows and a proper privy. We'll fish in mountain streams for trout as big as dogs, and someday we'll sit in rockers on the porch and reminisce about the silly old days when the stupid rotten sergeant blacked his eye, and how we made our great escape. Maybe on horseback, or in a silk balloon, I ain't decided which yet.

"It will be all right," I tell him. "Our Dear Mother always said things work out for the best."

Harold gives me a sorrowful look. "You were barely four

years old when Mother passed. How can you know what she said, or what she believed?"

"I know because you told me."

He nods to himself, as if he already knew what I would say. "I am sorry, Homer. I have let you down."

"Don't be silly. Squint sold you into the army. It ain't your fault."

"You don't understand," he says, sounding mournful. "I let it happen. I knew it was a sham, and could have said so before I joined the regiment. But I wanted to be shut of the farm, and our hard life. I wanted to breathe air that had never been dirtied by Squinton Leach."

"Oh," I say.

"There's worse." He hesitates, then takes a deep breath and continues. "For once in my life I wanted not to have to take care of you. Not to be your brother and your mother and your father all rolled into one. I wanted out, Homer. I saw my chance and took it."

Poor Harold looks so miserable I can't hardly stand it. Besides, the things he's telling me don't exactly come as a big surprise. I sort of knew it all along, that he wanted to get away from Squint, and not to always be having to look after his little brother.

I say, "It don't matter because you don't have to take care of me no more. It's my turn to take care of you."

Harold studies me and shakes his head and smiles a little. "How'd you get here, really? A boy your age that never left the farm?"

I'm about to tell him the story of my true adventures, and all the fun and sorrows I had along the way, when an officer starts shouting out commands.

"Men of the Twentieth Maine, move out! We are shifting to the left! Keep formation! Keep formation!"

The guards kick me out of the prisoner wagon, but chase me no farther than a few yards. It is easy enough to follow as the regiment picks up and moves, along with the rest of the brigade.

There are thousands of soldiers below the crest of the hill, awaiting orders. Men from Maine and New York, Pennsylvania and Vermont, Massachusetts and Connecticut, Michigan and Illinois, and just about everywhere in the Northern states. The sound of rifle and artillery fire coming from the other side of the ridge is more or less continuous, and the men seem eager to join the fight.

This is the day, they tell one another. Today we stand our ground. Today we turn the tables on Robert E. Lee. Today we win the war.

I feel like tugging on sleeves and saying don't be in such a hurry, the bullets are faster than you. But I keep my mouth shut and my eyes on the prisoner wagon, trying to scheme up a plan to break Harold out of his confinement.

A little while later I see the wounded being carried back from the top of the hill, and it comes to me that maybe being a prisoner and mutineer ain't such a bad thing to be. Nobody's shooting at them. Could be worse.

Then worse himself comes charging up on a big gray

horse. Colonel Joshua Lawrence Chamberlain, the young commander of the 20th Maine, all fitted out with his sword and pistols and his fancy big mustache, and his eyes glowing like he's been to Heaven and seen the other side.

"Men of the Twentieth, look to me! See that small hill?" He points with his sword. "We must hold that with our lives! It guards the left of the Union Army and cannot be allowed to fall into rebel hands! Every man! Every man on the double! Run for the hill and take position! Follow the flag! Quickly now!"

He makes to wheel away and then thinks better of it. Instead he sidles up to the prisoners and shows them the flat of his sword, tapping it against his boot. "Gentlemen! Those willing to fight will get a good word from me. Obey your orders and I'll do my best to get the charges dropped."

To my dismay, the prisoners stand as one, including my brother, Harold Figg, begging to be allowed to fight.

The guards release them, and they dust away the *M* so cruelly chalked upon their uniforms. The prisoners and guards grab rifles and cartridge boxes and run for the hill, following the flag of the 20th Maine.

All is confusion, but I manage to get to Harold just as he picks up a rifle.

"Now's our chance!" I say. "There's no one to stop us! We can run for it! We'll be miles away before they notice!"

Harold looks at me like I got two heads. "I gave my word," he says.

"Words won't stop the bullets!" I say as he wrenches

himself loose from my grasp. "Words won't keep the shells from exploding! Words won't stop you getting killed and leaving me alone in this world!"

He shoves me to the ground.

"Stay there!" he orders me. "Crawl under the wagon and keep yourself safe. I will see you after the battle, Homer, after the fight is done."

Then he's running up the hill, a rifle in one hand and a cartridge pouch in the other.

"Harold, stop!"

He won't stop. He keeps on going, running toward the sound of gunfire.

What choice do I have? I haven't come all this way for nothing. So I follow my brother up the hill, into the fight, into the Battle of Gettysburg.

35

EVEN WHEN THEY'RE DEAD

THE TOP OF THE LITTLE HILL is strewn with rocks and boulders and a few spindly trees. The men from the 20th Maine spread out along the ridge, quickly finding shelter among the rocks. From here they may fire down upon the enemy and still be afforded some small protection.

They don't have long to wait. Ten minutes after occupying the hill a full regiment of Alabama men attack from below, waving their regimental flag.

Suddenly gray uniforms swarm among the rocks and into the open, surging upward with that terrible cry that is called a rebel yell. The *ki-yi yip-yip* of the rebel yell being partways an owl-like screech and partways a high-pitched yelp that makes your skin crawl if you happen to be on the receiving end.

The bullets start flying before I can locate Harold or find a place to hide. Bullets spitting off rocks and scudding up the dirt and making little smacking noises as they hit skinny trees that are too small to hide behind.

Everywhere I turn there are more bullets striking all around, like hornets swarming, *snick-snick-snick*.

Finally Harold scoots out from behind his rock and drags me to safety. "What are you doing, you little fool? Do you want to be killed, is that it?" he asks, panting.

"I want to go home."

Harold grunts, then takes aim between the rocks and fires his Springfield rifle. His leather cartridge pouch lies open at his side and he swings the rifle around, tears the paper cartridge in his teeth, rams it down the muzzle, swings the rifle back around, inserts the primer cap, and cocks the hammer—all as quick as you can count.

Then he takes careful aim and fires and does it all over again.

There are forty cartridges in his leather pouch, which means when he fires thirty-seven more times he'll be out of ammunition. Figure twenty minutes or less, if he keeps up to speed.

"Where are you going?" he cries.

"To get more ammunition!"

And that's what I do, scampering down the back slope of the hill, out of the line of fire. I follow the others and locate the powder wagons, hoisting a wooden ammunition box that looks like a little casket and dragging it up to where Harold is still loading and firing his rifle, steady as a clock, a bullet fired every count of twenty.

After seeing that Harold is well supplied, I make myself useful hauling ammunition to some of the others, who are strung out all the way to the southern end of the little hill, and under vicious fire from the troops below.

Time and again the Alabama men scream out their wild rebel yell and swarm up the hill, only to be turned back at the last moment, punished by the men of the 20th Maine, who hold their ground, hunkered down among the rocks like smoking barnacles, refusing to let go.

For an hour or more the bullets fly. Men are wounded, men scream, men die, but still the bullets fly.

Colonel Chamberlain is everywhere. He strides along the ridge, in direct line of the rebel sharpshooters firing from below, ordering where his men should be placed and how they might best repel the next desperate charge of the troops from Alabama.

Bullets crease the air around him, close enough to part his hair, but he never flinches from his purpose.

Later I heard he was a college professor who knew nothing of war excepting what he'd read in books, but that fateful day upon the little hill he seems to be Napoleon himself, never in doubt as to what must happen next. He orders where the men should move, when the line should be extended, and when the wounded should be dragged back to safety and carried by stretcher away from the withering fire.

The bodies of the fallen have to be left where they fall, to be retrieved when the battle concludes, if ever it does.

Even when they're dead, bullets make them flinch.

Seeing me scurrying along with a load of ammunition, Colonel Chamberlain pauses in his purposeful stride and says, "You there, boy! Do you know the risk you take?"

"Yes, sir!"

"Very good! Carry on!" he commands. "And keep your head down!"

Then his attention is drawn elsewhere as one of his officers falls, wounded in the neck, and he must see to a replacement.

In the first few minutes of the assault the rebels almost gain the top of the hill, where they are met with pistol shot and sword. A few soldiers fight hand to hand, rolling among the rocks, each one desperate to kill the other man, but most of the casualties are inflicted at a distance of thirty yards or so. An Alabama man will emerge from cover, firing as he tries to gain a few yards, and a Maine man will stand up, exposed to the withering hail of bullets, and take aim at the Alabama man, and most times one or the other will fall wounded or dead.

Sometimes both.

All to gain advantage on a rocky little spur of a hill that happens to stand at the far end of the line, where the Confederates hope to sweep around and crush the Union Army from both sides. A small hill shrouded in gray gun smoke and running with the blood of the wounded and the dead.

The steady hail of lead chops little bits out of the trees, like they are being attacked by small, invisible axes.

I keep down, like Harold and the colonel suggested, and find myself a good boulder to hide behind.

All the ammunition has been taken from the wagons and distributed. It can't last forever, the way the men are using it up, each taking two or three shots a minute, but for now the gunfire spits and pops like a full load of popcorn in a hot pan of grease.

There comes a lull when only a few guns are popping off and I hear Harold call out for more ammunition.

"All gone!" an officer shouts back. "Find cartridges where you can!"

Already they are borrowing cartridge cases from the many who have fallen. The dead men don't object.

In my hiding place, curled up small, I'm praying the cartridges will run out soon, so we can fall back.

It comes to this: I care not if the rebels take the hill. There are a million hills in Pennsylvania, let them have this one if they want it so bad!

A little distance away, half obscured by the clouds of gun smoke, the colonel confers with his officers. From what I can see of their faces the news must be very grim indeed.

Good, I'm thinking, sound your retreat! An army can't fight without bullets, can it? We are outnumbered, outgunned, and outfought. The only sensible thing to do is run for it.

Then, clear as a bell that tolls through the fog, comes his order.

"Fix bayonets!" he roars.

All down the line soldiers eagerly slip bayonets onto the muzzles of their empty rifles and ready themselves for what happens next.

Ahead of me, crouching behind his rock, my brother, Harold, shakes his head at me.

"Homer, get back!" he shouts above the din. "Go home! Save yourself!"

Then Colonel Chamberlain's voice booms out, louder than the crack of artillery.

"Charge!" he commands, lifting high his sword.

Harold leaps to his feet and follows him down the hill, into the guns of the enemy.

———

To this day I cannot say what made me follow my brother down that hill. It was not ignorance, because I had seen what war does, and hated it. It was not courage, because fear of dying made me scream out loud.

All I know is, there I was, running after Harold and begging him to take shelter. And as I come over the top of the hill the air itself is hot enough to catch afire from the heat of flying lead.

To my shock, no more than fifty feet separates us from the enemy. Measured in blood it might as well be a hundred miles. All around me men are charging downhill, eyes wide in the madness of killing, teeth snapping like dogs at the scent of death.

Fast as I'm running over that rough ground, I can't seem

to catch up to Harold. Soldiers on either side of him fall like rag dolls but he keeps on going.

Just ahead of him is the burly sergeant with the regimental flag, the one who cussed Harold and said he was swamp trash. The sergeant stumbles, clutching at his stomach, and the flag starts to fall.

Without breaking stride Harold drops his empty rifle and seizes the flag from the wounded sergeant.

"Harold, no!"

Now all rebel eyes—and rebel guns—will be upon him. My brother holds up the flag as he advances, leaning into the lead-filled air as if he is leaning into warm summer rain.

"Harold, get down!" I scream. "Get down or be killed!"

Holes appear like stars in the billowing flag, but still he will not take shelter.

I search for a rock to throw at him, to bring him to his senses, but the first thing my groping hand encounters is the fallen sergeant who passed the flag to Harold. He lies on his side, grinning at his pain, hands clawing at his wounded stomach. I want to ask him why he blacked my brother's eye, and if he's sorry now, but it don't seem right to ask while he's busy dying.

Instead I lift the pistol from his holster and take aim, intending to fire at Harold's feet to get his attention.

I pull the trigger.

The bullet strikes the ground. Harold falls.

At first I think he has finally been struck by rebel lead and then I see what has happened. My own shot has splintered away a chunk of rock that has stuck itself in his leg like a dart in a board.

As Harold falls he tries to keep the flag upright.

Without thinking I drop the sergeant's pistol and somehow the flag ends up in my hands and my brother lying at my feet.

By rights I should toss aside the flag and drop to the ground and try to get under the flying lead, but something in me won't let go. Now that the flag is in my hands it don't seem right to let it fall on bloody ground.

A dumb idea. Dumb enough to get me killed, but there it is.

The strangest thing is happening. All around me, all down the hillside, rebel soldiers are throwing down their rifles and surrendering. Begging mercy from the crazy men with the bayonets, men mad enough to charge without a shot to fire, into the face of certain death. Men who will not give up. Men who would rather die than be defeated.

Beneath me Harold is groaning and trying to pry loose the sliver of stone imbedded in his leg. I am sorry he is hurt but glad that he is alive.

Then I notice that not all the Alabama soldiers have surrendered. I notice because one of them has risen from the ground with his sword in both hands. His eyes moving from the flag to me, as if deciding what to strike first, the hated Yankee flag or the boy holding it.

He hesitates.

At that moment exactly, Colonel Joshua Lawrence Chamberlain appears and aims his pistol at the swordsman's head with a steady hand.

"Surrender or die," he suggests.

The man drops the sword and falls to his knees.

"I'll take the flag," the colonel says. "See to your brother."

36

WHAT HAPPENED IN THE END

THAT DAY THE BATTLE ends for us, but not for others.

All that night, as I waited in the surgeon's tent with Harold, the wounded were carried from the field. Supplies were brought in, meals were cooked or eaten cold, artillery cannons were shifted into new positions. Men sang and cried and waited for the dawn. And when the sun rose it did not seem so bad at first. A few skirmishes, a cannonade or two—it was as if the rebels wanted only to give us a little slap, to remind us they had not been truly beaten.

Then, early that afternoon, the Confederate artillery began to fire in earnest, hurling thousands of explosive shells upon the Union positions, and the earth itself began to shake, as if some mad giant was stamping his feet in rage.

Our tent was more than a mile from the field of battle but the shaking was so bad that water sloshed in the glass and dust rose from the ground. One of the surgeons shouted that it was like an earthquake, but unlike an earthquake it did not stop.

Eventually, of course, it did stop, and the Confederates, thinking the Union artillery had been pounded into oblivion, launched an infantry attack into the very middle of the Union forces. They sent almost thirteen thousand men marching in line across a mile of open ground. And in that bloody mile, pounded by Union artillery and hundreds of Union sharpshooters, half of the Confederates were killed or wounded.

Among those who participated in that doomed assault was Reginald Robertson Crockett, the gentleman spy, the man I knew as Professor Fleabottom. Having bribed his way free of his jailers, paying them with the golden buttons on his coat, he rode hard for the battlefield and soon perished there, as his famous ancestor did at the Alamo, fighting to the last man.

That night Robert E. Lee and his rebel army fled south, and would never again set foot on Northern soil.

A FEW DAYS AFTER the battle, while the dead were still being buried in the fields and meadows of Gettysburg, and some of their fallen officers shipped home in boxes, Colonel Chamberlain came to see us. Harold's wound was healing nicely, so it seemed, and the colonel had sent a telegraph message to Pine Swamp, Maine, and received a reply.

Harold's age was proved as seventeen.

"You are released from your service as being too young to enlist," the colonel informed him.

Better words I never heard, although Harold was none too pleased—he wanted to keep on fighting, once his leg had healed.

Before he left us the colonel turned to me and asked why I did it. Why did I stand my ground and hold the flag?

"You're only a boy and could have run away with no shame," he says, fixing his cold blue eyes on me. "What made you stand?"

Try as I might, I could not think of an answer that day. And all these years later, I still cannot say why I did not run. Surely I wanted to, but something made me stay.

"If we are still fighting in two years' time," the colonel said, "I will send for both of you."

In two years time the long and terrible war finally came to an end, and we were never again called upon to fight. Instead we wandered north, relying upon each other, working wherever we could, on farms and in small factories, and searching all the while for a medicine show as good as Professor Fleabottom's.

We never did find one.

Eventually Jebediah Brewster located us in our wanderings and took us in and made us feel at home, and was made our legal guardian. By then the slaves had been freed of their bondage and the Brewster Mines were opened up again, bringing precious stones out of the dirt and rocks.

Mr. Brewster says me and Harold are like tourmaline.

We come in dirty but we wash up shiny, and he is proud to call us his kin and make us his heirs. It was him that suggested I write down my true adventures, so if you hate this book put the blame on Jebediah Brewster, not on me.

One more thing I got to say about my big brother, Harold, and that's what happened after the battle at Gettysburg. At first his wound healed, and for a few weeks it seemed like his leg would be saved. Then one day an infection set in, and it swelled up blue and nearly killed him. Nothing to cure it but the knife and the saw.

My brother lost his leg.

He still feels it sometimes, like the ghost of a limb that used to be. When that happens he will smile and say, "Remember when we were boys? Remember how you saved my life by trying to kill me? Remember how you stood your ground, a small boy of twelve that never owned a pair of shoes? Don't you worry, little brother, don't you shed a tear. Wasn't you that took my leg, it was the war."

I think in some ways it's like that for all of us, living with the ghosts of things that used to be, or never were. We're all of us haunted by yesterday, and we got no choice but to keep marching into our tomorrows.

Keep marching, boys and girls. Keep marching.

YOURS TRULY (MOSTLY),

HOMER P. FIGG

Some Additional Civil War Facts, Opinions, Slang & Definitions, to be Argued, Debated & Cogitated Upon

ABOLITIONIST
One who wants to abolish the institution of slavery.

ABRAHAM LINCOLN
The prairie lawyer whose election as president prompted many of the slave-holding states to declare that they were no longer part of the United States of America, and would form a nation of their own. The new Confederacy struck quickly, attacking Fort Sumter a mere thirty-nine days after Lincoln took office. Lincoln's own view that slavery should not be expanded into the new states—a view that failed to prevent war—eventually evolved into the belief that slavery itself should be abolished. His short speech honoring the dead at Gettysburg is considered to be one of the most powerful and eloquent in the English language. He was assassinated a few days after the Confederacy surrendered.

ARTILLERY
Cannons and big guns, some with ranges of more than a mile. Arguably the most effective cannon used in the Civil War was the Napoleon, which fired a twelve-pound exploding shell loaded with small iron balls. It was, in effect, a giant sawed-off shotgun.

BALLOONS

Large silk surveillance balloons filled with hydrogen gas. The advantage of height enabled pilots to survey the entire battlefield and report to the generals. After a time the opposing army learned how to shoot down the balloons, and their use was discontinued.

BASEBALL

Sometimes called "town ball" or "bat ball," it was encouraged by the army to improve physical conditioning. Teamwork on the field was thought to lead to teamwork on the field of battle. Organized baseball grew in popularity after the soldiers returned from war.

CASUALTIES OF THE CIVIL WAR

More than 600,000 lives were lost, the most in any war fought by American soldiers.

CONDUCTORS

Men and women, often of color, who guided slaves to freedom.

CONSCRIPTION LAW

Required all males between the ages of twenty and forty-five to register for the draft by April 1, 1863. A man could be exempted by paying three hundred dollars or by hiring a substitute to serve in his place.

EMANCIPATION PROCLAMATION

Lincoln's executive order on January 1, 1863, freeing slaves in the Confederate states. Slaves in the border states of West Virginia, Kentucky, Missouri, Maryland, and Delaware would not finally be freed until the war ended.

FIREARMS

The rifled musket — soon shortened to "rifle" — was the most common firearm of the Civil War. It fired a new lead slug developed by French army Captain Claude Minié. Often called a "minié ball," this modern half-inch bullet was made to spin by the rifling inside the barrel of the weapon, which greatly improved accuracy. It could be deadly at a range of half a mile, and changed the nature of warfare. The author refers to this new form of ammunition simply as a bullet, for clarity.

FREDERICK DOUGLASS

One of the most amazing men of the 19th century, Douglass secretly taught himself to read while laboring as a slave in Maryland. When he began to teach other slaves to read, fearful slave owners menaced him with clubs and stones. After several attempts, he finally escaped to freedom in 1838, at the age of twenty. Soon after, he was asked to speak at an abolitionist meeting, and his powerful eloquence and intellect made him one of the most celebrated orators and authors of his age. He championed the rights of all humans — whether black, female, Native American, or recent immigrant — until the day of his death in 1895.

FUGITIVE SLAVE LAW

Meant that escaped slaves could be seized and returned to their "owners" without trial, relying only on the word of the owner. There were many instances in which legally freed blacks and some who had been born free were "returned" in this way. The Fugitive Slave Law outraged many Americans, even those not opposed to slavery itself.

GEEK

Carnival performer who bites off the heads of live chickens.

JEFFERSON DAVIS

President of the Confederate States of America, 1861–1865. In stating his reasons for going to war, Davis wrote, "What is the reason we are compelled to assert our rights? That the labor of our African slaves should be taken away by the federal government." His vice-president, Alexander Stephens, was even more forthright: "The immediate cause of our present revolution is the threat to the institution of slavery. Our new government is founded upon the great truth that the Negro is not equal to the white man, that slavery, subordination to the superior race, is his natural and moral condition."

Lincoln-Douglas Debates
In 1858, Abraham Lincoln had a series of debates with Stephen A. Douglas. Both men were running for the U.S. Senate and had passionate, opposing views. Lincoln favored banning slavery in the new states and territories. Douglas favored the rights of states to keep slavery legal if they so chose. Their speeches were carried in newspapers and avidly read by thousands of interested citizens. Douglas won the senate seat, but Lincoln became famous for his eloquence and went on to be elected president in 1860.

Medicine Show
A traveling entertainment show, often from a horse-drawn wagon, featuring music and performances of all kinds. The purpose of the free show was to attract customers for elixirs and bottled medicines.

New Ways of Waging War
The American Civil War saw the first appearance of the following: steel ships, effective submarines, aerial reconnaissance balloons, military telegraph systems, the periscope (used to peer out of trenches), landmine fields, electrically exploded mines and bombs, the Gatling machine gun, flame throwers, long-range rifles, battle photographs, the conscription of men into the army, the Medal of Honor.

Privy
A small shack or closet that served as a bathroom, often located some distance from the house.

Quakers
Also known as the Religious Society of Friends. Quakers believe that humans should strive for simplicity, equality, and integrity,

and should not engage in violence or war. In this book, a version of American Quaker 'plain speech' is spoken by Mr. Brewster.

RAILROADS
Crucial to the war for both sides. Many soldiers were transported near the battlefield by steam engine. Trains carried supplies and ammunition. Destruction of enemy trains and tracks was a high priority of both armies.

SLAVE CATCHERS
Bounty hunters who had the legal right to seize and transport fugitive slaves, returning them to their owners.

TELEGRAPH
Messages, signals, and orders were electrically transmitted by Morse code through thousands of miles of telegraph wires maintained by the Union Army.

WAR
The means by which tribes, clans, groups, and nations settle their differences by killing one another. The Civil War began in 1861 and ended in 1865.

CIVIL WAR SLANG

ARKANSAS TOOTHPICK: a long knife

BEEHIVE: a backpack

BIG BUGS: important people

BILLY YANK: a Union soldier

BREAD BAG: a supply bag worn over the shoulder; a haversack

BUMBLE BEES: bullets

BUMMER: a soldier who deliberately lags behind

CABBAGING: stealing

DOG ROBBER: a cook

FIRE AND FALL BACK: vomit in fear

Forty dead men: forty rounds of ammo in the cartridge box

Fresh fish: new recruits

Go boil your shirt: take a hike; get lost

Grab a root: eat

Gunboats: army shoes

Horse collar: a blanket roll

Johnny Reb: a Confederate soldier

Layouts; coffee coolers: those who avoided battle

Let 'er rip: bring it on

Lucifers: matches

Muggins: a scoundrel

Old Scratch: the Devil

Opening the ball: begin the battle

Peddle lead: shoot fast

Pie eater: a boy from the country

Rag out: dress well

Quick step: diarrhea

Sharp operator: someone who could sell manure to a stable; swindler

Shin plasters: paper money

Showing the white feather: cowardice

Squash molished: a soldier with a hangover

Somebody's darlin': an unidentified corpse

Sow belly: bacon

Spondulix: money

Top rail: first class

Traps or trappings: a soldier's possessions

Weevil fodder: hardtack

Wrathy: angry